The Undocumented Americans

Catalina

CATALINA

CATALINA

A Novel

Karla Cornejo Villavicencio

ONE WORLD

NEW YORK

Published in the United States by One World, an imprint of Random House, a division of Penguin Random House LLC, New York.

ONE WORLD and colophon are registered trademarks of Penguin Random House LLC.

LIBRARY OF CONGRESS CATALOGING-IN-PUBLICATION DATA
Names: Cornejo Villavicencio, Karla, author.
Title: Catalina: a novel / by Karla Cornejo Villavicencio.
Description: First edition. | New York: One World, 2024.
Identifiers: LCCN 2023050448 (print) | LCCN 2023050449 (ebook) |
ISBN 9780593449097 (hardcover; acid-free paper) |
ISBN 9780593449103 (ebook)
Subjects: LCGFT: Novels.
Classification: LCC PS3603.O76453 C38 2024 (print) |
LCC PS3603.O76453 (ebook) | DDC 813/.6—dc23/eng/20231101
LC record available at https://lccn.loc.gov/2023050448
LC ebook record available at https://lccn.loc.gov/2023050449

Printed in the United States of America on acid-free paper

oneworldlit.com
randomhousebooks.com

2 4 6 8 9 7 5 3 1

First Edition

Book design by Caroline Cunningham
Title page and part title background art: iStock/oasis15

FOR TED AND MARCO

You know what you did.

PART ONE

SUMMER

In the summer of 2010, the year Instagram launched, there was a cricket invasion in Queens. Something to do with global warming and, if you believed my grandfather, yet another sign that America was lagging behind Cuba in scientific advances. He was not a communist, he just had a bit of a thing for Fidel. Dozens of crickets were under the floors and in the walls of our apartment. The landlord sent an exterminator, but it had little effect on their fornication. The sound was intolerably loud. My grandfather said that back in Ecuador, summer nights in Esmeraldas were so loud, it sounded like, well, what it was—a beach and a jungle. I had not been to Esmeraldas, where he spent every summer as a child. Like him, I was undocumented, so I could not go to Esmeraldas, probably ever. I would probably never see the Amazon, and thus I would never really know a summer night. He would always have that over me. He knew in his flesh what I could only read about and I read a lot.

As a kid, I read for escape, and nothing could be further from watching a cockroach lay dozens of tiny eggs on the kitchen sink than Jay Gatsby and his amorous preoccupations. I could relate to some of it—his immigrant hunger and interminable longing; I'd been to Long Island—but the lives of Nick and Daisy and Jordan were incomprehensible to me. I didn't understand what they wanted or why they wanted what they wanted. Their main problem seemed to be boredom. The cannon was white noise, and it was perfect.

I spent that summer, which was the summer before my senior year at Harvard, interning at America's third-most-prestigious literary magazine. Does that sound like a setup for a romantic comedy? I thought so, too. My expectations were high. During my commute, every single morning, on the L train between Bushwick and Manhattan, I just had a feeling Woody Allen was going to discover me. Rosario Dawson had been discovered on her stoop on the Lower East Side as a teenager. Charlize Theron was discovered at a bank. Toni Braxton was discovered at a gas station. I needed to be discovered because I wanted to get out of where I was, and according to Jay Gatsby and Joseph Kennedy, Sr., and Theodore Dreiser and Jay-Z, I could do it by becoming a star. It was a long shot but so was everything. If I didn't commit to *Catalina, Catalina, Catalina,* I would die of tuberculosis two decades ago, another uninsured girl at Bellevue known only by her wristband. If at any point I stopped believing, the spell would break. To be clear, it was Woody Allen who would discover me because he was a local. Almodóvar lives in Spain, and Sofia Coppola might find me too busty. Plus, if there was someone looking for muses on the train and if that muse was going to be a very young girl, for the verisimilitude of the thought exercise, it had to be Woody Allen.

Four years at Harvard had been presented to me like a trip to Disney World to a terminally ill child and the end was coming. I could not be legally employed after graduation. Don't get me wrong, I wasn't legally able to work that summer, either, but my lack of papers did not matter because unpaid internships did not pay and I only applied to unpaid internships. Employers argued it was not "work." Usually, the only people who could afford to do that sort of thing—move to New York for at least three months and live there without making an income—came from some kind of money, which kept that world small. But so long as I was enrolled in school and lived with my grandparents, I could do as many unpaid internships in media as I wanted. They could be like Pokémon cards.

I loved newspapers and magazines as a child. I was the perfect age for *Highlights for Children* when I came to America, and within a couple of years I graduated to *Reader's Digest* and then a couple of years after that I moved on to *Time*. By high school I was stealing old copies of *The New Yorker* from the school library. I had favorite writers (Alma Guillermoprieto for *The New York Review of Books*) and favorite publications (the *Oxford American*). I had opinions about paywalls and subscription models and the sustainability of relying on billionaire benefactors. But my love for American periodicals was not why I wanted to be a writer.

If you think about it, I never really even had a chance. I was named after the old Manuel Vallejo song "La Catalina," so I've known the tacky-sweet suet of self-protagonism since I was a little baby bird. I grew up with a soft spot for songs named after girls. I liked "Roxanne" by the Police, "Allison" by the Pixies, "Arabella" by the Arctic Monkeys, "Julia" by the Beatles, "Michelle" by the Beatles, "Lovely Rita" by the Beatles. There's a picture I saw on Tumblr of Bianca Jagger backstage at a Rolling Stones show. It's actually a picture of her foot in a white platform sandal; tucked into one of the straps is a backstage pass with her name on it. Whatever that was—I wanted to be that. Not Bianca Jagger. Not Mick Jagger. I wanted to be the photograph. I wanted to be *Art*. I knew it was only a matter of time before a boy in a band wrote a song about me, but that would require patience and I suspected the song would not be very good. Once again, I would have to rely on my own scruples to make things happen. I would have to become a writer myself.

I was on Tumblr since the beginning and eventually started writing myself, a blog that developed a small but devoted following of readers. I mostly wrote about music and made annotated breakup playlists for celebrity couples on the rocks, like Meg White and Jack White, and J.Lo and Ben Affleck. After that, I wanted to move up in the world, to blogs attached to iconic institutions like *Interview* magazine and *The Atlantic*. I pitched them coldly using emails I'd guessed from mastheads and did not lie about my age but did not volunteer it. I started covering shows, which gave me entry into twenty-one-plus venues because my name was on the press list. If you think I did not gallop like a newborn pony to the bouncer to say I should be on the guest list with the intended affect of a young Katharine Hepburn, you don't know Catalina Ituralde!

My grandparents supported my efforts. They had their suspicion of worldly gatherings and entertainments but I told them, had shown them in my heavily highlighted copy of *The Fiske Guide to Getting into the Right College*, that I needed to have extracurricular activities to impress admissions committees. That's all it took. My grandma helped me pick out what to wear to shows, and if I got out after midnight, my grandfather picked me up right outside the venue. It was all very wholesome. The three of us were a family that did things together.

The summer of the cricket invasion my grandparents both walked me to the Myrtle Avenue train station every morning.

From there, I took the train to my internship in Greenwich Village, and my grandfather took a different train to his job at a construction site in Midtown. My grandmother speed-walked back home, determined to miss as little of *Live with Regis and Kelly* as possible.

I have long since forgotten the names of the other summer interns except for Camilo Oliveres. We met when the internship director ushered us into the kitchen on the first day to explain that she had an honorary title to split between us. It was named after a slain *El Diario* editor who was killed by a Colombian crime boss at a restaurant in Jackson Heights. There was no money involved, no special duties or honors or responsibilities. The only stipulation was that the recipient be Latine.

"I'll step aside if that's okay," Camilo said. He spoke English with a Mexico City accent. I wondered if he could place mine. I blushed.

"Catalina, how about you?" the internship director asked. "Can we give this to you?"

"That sounds great, thanks," I said.

Technically, only I was Latine. Camilo, I would learn, was Latin American. His parents were psychoanalysts from Spain who fled Franco's persecution of leftist dissidents and resettled in Mexico, where they had him. He looked like he could be anything but he was Spaniard by blood and Mexican by birth. This allowed him to take certain liberties with me, for example, to speak to me in Spanish. When we walked back to the intern pen—that's what it was called, the intern pen—Camilo motioned for me to walk before him and said, a bit songsongy, *licenciada*. It was a layered inside joke, requiring a lot of assumptions he was not wrong about, among them, that I was not to be taken seriously.

The magazine's music editor had been recently fired, so I was assigned instead to Jim Young, the literary editor. Jim was partial to young women, not in a lascivious way necessarily—it was a matter of preserving the delicate balance of his ego. My job consisted of reading all the unsolicited short-story submissions the magazine received and passing any promising ones to Jim— rarely, very rarely. The magazine got a lot of letters from prisoners, and I always sent them copies of the magazine. Whenever I asked Jim to do something menial, like sign a contract or respond to an agent's query, I suspected I was taking editing time away from his writers, famously difficult men who wrote tens of thousands of words about being sad and horny, writers who couldn't spare the editing sessions.

When Jim passed by the intern pen, he'd greet me by asking, "Found any diamonds in the rough?"

"No," I said each time. "Not yet."

I looked around the office starry-eyed. Truman Capote had once walked down these very halls. It was the closest I had ever come to writers, real writers. *Artists*. The notion that writers might be actual people was as distant and existentially confusing to me as the concept of an infinite universe—definitely real, definitely there, but not something I could ascertain for myself or otherwise materially experience. There's magic in that. Writers were like the Greek gods, storied and problematic, and their corresponding mythologies fascinated me and kept me company. Emily Dickinson wasn't a real person, not really. This is why it was personally world-destroying for me when Jeffrey Eugenides visited Harvard my junior year.

Allegedly, after his professional engagement at *The Harvard Advocate* Eugenides went out with some members of the editorial board and hung out, vibed, smoked pot. Undergrads were breathing the same air, exchanging spittle and fungi spore with one of the great novelists of our time. I never stopped hearing

about it, or the couch on which he'd sat—was it a futon?—talking
about Radiohead. Magnanimous of the man with the mind that
brought forth *Middlesex* to also possess the heart to volunteer his
time with artsy college kids. We had long aged out of being pre-
cocious, and we all tried so hard. A litter of children and their
god.

Of course, he was my god, too. I even loved the way *Eugenides*
felt in my mouth, the way *Lo-lee-ta* felt in Humbert Humbert's,
but I wanted to think about him, I didn't want us to be friends. I
lived in the real world, and the real world was sad, and he lived in
literature, and literature was beautiful. Meeting him, talking to
him, seeing that he might leave his fly unzipped, that he might
have spinach in his teeth, that he might enjoy the attention of
nineteen-year-olds, I couldn't bear the possibility.

Before I came to New York City to live with my grandparents,
I lived in a small city in Ecuador called Cotopaxi, where my parents died when I was a baby and where my aunt and uncle raised
me until I was old enough to read, walk, and talk. Then, when I
was five years old, I was sent to live with my grandparents, who
were already in America. Up to that point, I'd never even met my
grandparents. All I knew about them is that they lived in New
York. All they really knew about me is that I survived the car
crash that killed my parents. I don't know how I survived. No one
knows. "This is a miracle," said the first police officer on the scene
of the crash. But nobody just *survives*. People are spared. God
has His reasons. The local papers ran the same picture—a baby
wrapped in a yellow blanket in the arms of a firefighter—and the
same headline: MILAGRO EN COTOPAXI.

The first few weeks with my grandparents were rough. They
cried into my hair a lot, holding each other, holding on to me like
a comfort item, a teddy bear, a blankie. They were distraught

over the fact I did not stop asking for my aunt and uncle, and even more distraught that I was calling my aunt "mami" and my uncle "papi." They asked me, repeatedly, to now call *them* mami and papi. I refused. Could my aunt and uncle have trained me to do exactly this to get under my grandparents' skin, just to prove their ownership over me? Well, my grandparents wouldn't put it past them! They got on the phone and had loud fights with my aunt and uncle using a calling card until time ran out and the call dropped, a built-in dramatic slam of the receiver. But mostly, they petted me and cried. At night, I locked myself in the bathroom but who was I kidding? I was five years old. I didn't know how to kill myself.

When I was in Ecuador, I had a thing about walking into traffic. My grandparents heard these stories from my aunt and uncle: If I was left alone, I walked outside and wandered into traffic. I was promised lots of little chocolates if I stopped, but I couldn't be bought. A few months after I arrived, my grandfather and I were on our way to the supermarket and when he looked away for one moment, a car had to slam its breaks to avoid hitting me. My grandfather was on the sidewalk, screaming, his hands over his mouth. I had been spared, again.

Throughout my childhood, I ruminated intensely on why I was brought to America. Nobody had explained it to me. I wanted to know why my aunt and uncle did not want me living with them anymore, if in fact that's what happened. Perhaps my grandparents sent for me. Perhaps they were getting old and realized that if they raised me, I might take care of them when they were no longer able to work in this country. That seems like a cynical calculation but I understood the role cynical calculations play in survival. Simply asking somehow always felt off the table. But one day, my grandmother was detangling my hair with a wide-tooth comb while I sat cross-legged on my bed. My straight black hair fell to my waist and taking care of it—combing it, braiding it, trimming my ends—was something we did together. I felt close to her, so I just went for it.

"Abuela, why did I leave Ecuador?" I asked really fast so I had no time to stop myself.

"Hija. Don't bring up Ecuador, they're listening," my grandmother said.

"Who is?"

"They monitor everything, Catalina. They track everything. They listen to our phone calls, they have our houses bugged. They know every book we check out of the library."

I laughed. "The *government*?"

She did not respond. I did not stop laughing.

"Wait, Grandma, the American government or the Ecuadorian government?"

My giggling was contagious and soon my grandmother was laughing, too. I leaned over to tickle her and she slapped my hand away. She cleared her throat and composed herself.

"We all knew you would have better educational opportunities here," she said, working the comb through a knot, "and now you can be anything you set your mind to."

That was their story and they stuck to it.

I remember very little of my time in Ecuador—playing water games with my cousins during Carnaval, eating crab in Guayaquil. I was born in a city named after a volcano, and I've deluded myself into thinking I can remember the way the volcano looked outside the window at dusk—in my few memories of Ecuador, it is always dusk. The Cotopaxi, my snowcapped birthstone, is the highest active volcano in the world. When the volcano explodes, the lava will run downhill and cover the entire city, fill-ing both sides of the Pan-American Highway. The city has been rebuilt three times. The first terrible explosion was in 1742, and it destroyed everything. The survivors rebuilt the city. In 1863, there was another eruption. The survivors rebuilt the city. The third terrible eruption was in 1877. The city was once again rebuilt; the next eruption was in 2015. They rebuilt. The volcano has been quiet since then.

Everything I know about Latin America comes from my grandfather and this is what I've gathered: If a place in the world could be accused of being too much, of not taking off one item of clothing or accessories before leaving the house, of in general being the opposite of Coco Chanel, that is the Andes, which simultaneously houses rainforests, desert, mountains, beaches, and snow, cartels, and people who love Jesus so much that they put themselves through crucifixion.

My grandfather told me I had dimples because when I was born, my parents called an indigenous woman to come to the hospital and rub raw dry peas into my cheeks to form the indentations. It was their choice to make me beautiful. I was never told where this woman came from. How did they find her? Is this a service she provided widely? How much did she charge? The point of the story, in any case, is that I had been created.

While I was being created in the Andes, my grandparents were trying their damnedest to make a better life for themselves in America. My grandfather took great pride in his work, but as he felt himself age out of manual labor, he became dark and brooding about citizenship and the way it eluded him; he consulted all kinds of disque-lawyers and notarios about increasingly obscure paths toward a green card. My grandparents arrived in the country a few months after the cutoff date established in the 1986 amnesty law, and those few months haunted him for the rest of

his life. They had been so fucking close. It drove him mad when
other men, men like him, lesser men even, had lucky breaks and
a pathway toward citizenship opened up for them. My grandmother for her part refused to talk about our legal status at all.
After immigrating to America she worked as a seamstress in a
factory until her eyesight began to fail her. Now bespectacled,
she remained at home restlessly juggling the duties of a house-
wife with the ghosts of what could have been breathing down her
neck, never giving her a moment of peace.

My grandmother was a woman who wanted to work. She
wanted to work and have her own paycheck. She wanted to leave
the house every day with coffee in her thermos, wearing flats but
carrying pumps in her purse. It was apparent to everyone with
eyes that hers was not the life she dreamed of. My grandmother
babysat for neighbors and when the kids were over, playing in the
living room, watching PBS Kids, I saw her lean against the doorway as if in a trance. She was physically in the room but she was
not with us. I had some clues about who she might have been as
a girl. For example, I never saw my grandmother carry a baby.
Our congregation had a rotating door of adorable toddlers and
cherubic infants and everything in between and still she resisted.
I admired her for it, for refusing to perform maternal instinct in
front of demanding eyes she knew were trying to see it in her. I
wondered what kind of mom she was to my father, whether he
had ever noticed her thing with babies. I wondered how he felt
after my grandmother left him for America. He would have been
around fifteen.

I knew in my heart that anything I had done or could do in
America, my grandmother would have done more and better if
she had only had the opportunity. You're actually here to see her,
not me. My heart felt heavy under the weight of the dead little

girl with big Broadway dreams that I imagined was mummified inside my grandmother. I was a spoiled princess. I hadn't even had to cross the border. I came on a plane.

I noticed right away that my newfound grandparents carried an air of conspiracy about them, and I was convinced from the get-go that they were hiding things from me that would one day cause me great and surprising harm. So I made a point of searching the apartment whenever I could. My grandfather kept his secret possessions in the bottom drawer of his dresser, loose batteries and condoms. My grandma's stash of secret objects was in her underwear drawer—inside was nice makeup she didn't want me to find, the Chanel body lotion she lovingly acquired through a six-month layaway and that I was not allowed to use. And then there was a mysterious shoebox filled with papers in the closet, behind the winter sweaters. During those early years, I was incandescently curious about this secret box, fantasizing about papers in there that proved they were not my grandparents, that my parents were alive, that my parents would come pick me up and they would know what to do with me. But when the years passed without that happening, I resigned myself to the home and family I had been offered, thanked God for His blessings, and resolved to make them proud in the only way I knew how.

I didn't just have to get good grades, though. I had to get them in a way that set me apart from everyone else. Only that impressed my grandparents.

Getting the only A+.

79 but the only one that passed.

The first person to have ever gotten this question right.

A teary teacher grabbing their hands on report card night to say: no, don, doña, thank *you*.

Eventually, the arrival in America of their dead son's special little girl breathed some hustle back into my grandparents. Everyone needs a raison d'être. My grandparents were now positive that God set me aside to do something special. I had been spared so many times by unpredictable strikes of divine chance, goodness, and mirth, and on top of that had found in my throat, like a swollen lymph node, the gift of the Puritan tongue. Being an immigrant has always been a game of chance, and here I was before them, a lottery ticket.

My grandparents did a quiet math around me, balancing the reality of the present and all its dinginess with the possibility of a happier future. I tried very hard to make the sacrifice seem worth it. What was The Sacrifice? It was everything they did or went without to help me make it in America. My grandfather's job was demeaning and he did it for me. He did it for money but it was money for me. And not enough money, my grandmother would be the first to remind you. Being undocumented is not for the weak of heart. My grandparents lived hunched over, arms linked; climbing up in this world meant standing on their backs, and they let me know it. "All of this is for you," my grandfather would say as my grandmother massaged Tiger Balm into his hands. "As long as you get an education, everything will have been worth it."

The smell of my childhood is bleach and mulling spices; my grandmother was fastidious about keeping house, and she boiled cinnamon, clove, and star anise in a big pot over the gas stove to mask the constant smell of Clorox. It was cozy and bright and it made home smell like Christmas all year round. Still, she could do nothing about the fact that our apartment's walls were covered in paint of dubious origins and dime-size peeling flakes could fall on you while you were in the shower or taking a shit, bits of eggshell falling from the sky. She could also do nothing about the temperature of our home, which was always mind-numbingly wrong. The landlord controlled our heat. We opened the windows if the place got too stuffy and turned on the oven when it was too cold. This is not safe, but space heaters were out of the question. I was very scared of space heaters as a little girl. The Spanish news in winter is full of stories of the ghetto on fire, space heaters killing people who did not deserve to die, just nice normal people who were cold, god forbid. It occupied an outsized space in my mind; alternatively, it occupied a normal amount of space in my mind and it's everyone else who's crazy.

The air quality in our home was not good for me, and when I was twelve, my pediatrician said that I had asthma. I was aghast. I was born nine thousand feet above sea level! My lungs were supposed to be spectacular. Did my pediatrician not know? Who I was? Should we tell her?

My grandmother was born Fernanda Maldonado and when she married my grandfather Francisco, she took his last name. Ituralde. She was drawn to self-serious, charismatic men. She told me that as a girl, she played a game when she was around adults at neighborhood parties, scanning the room to determine who she needed to twirl for to stay alive a little while longer, so to speak. She'd walk in a room and try to identify the most powerful person there, which is how she learned to spot charlatans. It's hard to stop thinking like a prey animal. Best to never start, really.

My grandmother's father never acknowledged her and her mother never wanted her, so she was raised by an aunt and uncle. After twelve years as the top student at Sacred Heart of Jesus, a Catholic all-girls school run by nuns, she got the gist. She was an orphan, fine, she could do nothing about the fact that she was an orphan, but she could become a very famous orphan, perhaps the most famous orphan of all time. Out of all the orphans in the world, she could be their valedictorian.

I once saw the lady doing my grandma's hair make the sign of the cross after seeing the amount of bleach it would take to give her highlights. Her hair was a mousy brown at some point but she highlighted it every summer and explained that she got extra dimension and wave from all the chlorine from the YMCA pool. This had happened for so many summers, and each time so tastefully, imperceptibly done by the hard metals in the water and María at the salon, that like a well-worn sheepskin, the color it was now was the color it was meant to be, rich.

What you should know about my grandfather at the time he met my grandmother is that if there *was* such a thing—a ranking of orphans—he would want the very top orphan, the most orphaned one of all. My grandfather's job as a used car parts salesman in Ecuador required him to travel for weeks at a time. Whenever he visited her town, he threatened to steal her away and marry her. She was drawn to his hunger for adventure, his neck, the way he laced up his boots. She wanted to tell him that she felt everything he felt in his body in hers except she was a girl, but she couldn't bring herself to say it. Instead, she married him. There is only one photograph of them on their wedding day and they both look sad.

There's something about the faces of everyone in my family and in mine. I think you can see in our eyes the kind of sadness, which is in two places at once—mourning the past, grieving the future. Sad in a historically significant and visually satisfying way. Looking sad like it's your job.

My grandmother was spectacularly sensitive. She always needed to create a different world for herself because what was before her wouldn't do. When I arrived, she created new worlds for me, too. In the summers of my childhood, she set up a kiddie pool on the roof of our apartment building where we would sit cross-legged to fit across from each other, our bodies shiny with coconut oil. She hung white strings over my desk and around and above my bed, creating curtains and canopies and trains, and I crawled inside to read while she prepared tuna fish, curtido, and thick-cut french fries, a quick Ecuadorian coastal lunch.

One night when my grandparents thought I was sleeping, I overheard my grandmother telling my grandfather that she was scared about how barren the world was for girls like me.

"Look, Catalina is the fighting cock you put all your money on," my grandfather explained to my grandma in aggressive whispers that, as usual, leaned into New World–old country metaphors I could not fully comprehend. "It doesn't matter who they place in front of her, what cage she's put in, what country in the world she has to fight in, she's going to win because she is a gold-standard fighting cock."

But I was not a gold-standard fighting cock. I was just a girl. That part, the fact of my being just a girl, is something my grandmother never forgot and my grandfather seldom remembered.

Though I haven't lived under my grandfather's roof in well over a decade, I still feel a pit in my stomach every day, unfailingly, at dusk. My grandfather got out of work at 6:00 P.M. and was home by 7:00. I wanted my grandfather to not hurt; it was clear he was always in a deep, vinyl, disco pain that I couldn't understand but made me and my grandma run around like chickens with our heads cut off, keeping it moving, looking productive, because if we idled he might start yelling, spittling, might enter in soliloquy, his brow furrowed exactly as you know. Sometimes he would give us the silent treatment for four or five days but moved around the apartment, sharing a bathroom with us, awkwardly showing up at the shower at the same time as me, then scowling off. Since he wouldn't join us at the table, I would bring his meals to him in the living room. My grandmother estimated how long it would take him to eat his food, because if we took too long to go pick up the dishes, he'd then accuse us of forgetting him, not caring that he was this way, not caring about him at all, treating him like an ass, like a dog. So she guessed when he'd be done, and I went to retrieve the dishes.

"You could at least let your hair down," he'd say to my grandma before falling asleep on the couch. "I see women who have their hair down, who have makeup on, who have their nails done for their husbands. They still want to woo their husbands, as if they were boyfriends."

"I am not going to put on makeup and put on clothes to go out when I am stuck indoors, cleaning, cooking, doing the laundry. Do you want me to do that in heels?"

"Well, you look like a dyke," he said to her.

"For what it's worth, I think you look like Theodore Roosevelt," I interrupted.

"Oh my god, hija, what are you saying?" she said.

"You know the American president who was kind of fat and had a mustache and wore safari clothing?"

"No, Catalina, no, I don't," she said.

"Oh, come on, yes you do!" I insisted. "There's that bronze statue of him in front of the American Museum of Natural History. And another one inside, on a bench. Remember how you asked me to take a photo of you and that bronze statue?" She looked at me blankly.

"You were wearing that hat that I hate?"

She thought that was very funny. This was my job as a kid: to defuse the tension and lighten the mood. One of the first places I saw in America was the American Museum of Natural History. My grandparents took me a few days after I got off the plane. I had never looked upon a large North American mammal, and now before me was a grizzly bear on its hind legs. I felt shy.

For the occasion, my grandmother had worn what I can only now describe as a safari outfit. Tan pants, light olive shirt, a little white belt, a tan suede jacket, all procured at her famous Good-wills. (Famous to me, she goes to them a lot.) I saw that her outfit looked just like the man's in the statue. We passed by the first statue at the entrance of the building: Theodore Roosevelt on horseback, leading a Native American warrior on one side and an African warrior on the other side, trailing significantly behind him on foot, looking freaking honored to be supporting actors in the story Teddy told himself about himself. Positioned near the museum exit was another brass statue of Roosevelt, this time sitting on a bench. As soon as I laid eyes on him, I thought this Teddy, too, was dressed exactly like my grandmother. I was too shy to remark on this—I had just met my third set of parents and was doing my best to keep them. I was on my best behavior! But I couldn't hold in a laugh. She asked me what made me so happy and I've never been great at lying so I just told her.

"You're wicked," she said to me, eyes bright. It was the first thing she learned about me.

That was a long time ago. I had so much to learn about wicked-ness.

I have a question. You are a twenty-year-old girl walking home from the train station with a lollipop in your mouth or, if you prefer, eating a banana, catnip for run-of-the-mill men and their enthusiasm for phallic imagery. You don't know how women give blow jobs but you know how porn actresses give blow jobs, and that's the choreography straight men would have in their minds. How do you engage with the lollipop non-pornographically? It's not easy to do. If you leave the lollipop in your mouth for too long, to avoid interacting with it at all, you'll salivate, and at first you'll think that allowing the saliva to gather in your mouth is clever, that the passersby will only see the stick in your mouth, Clint Eastwood with a toothpick, but at some point you're going to have to swallow the pooling saliva, and the longer you wait, the harder you'll have to swallow. It might hurt. Or you might choke. You're making this very easy for me.

At the magazine, I generally kept to myself. The other interns were smart and nice to me, but we didn't hang out after work. I was intimidated by the girl interns. They didn't wear makeup and went to see people like Noam Chomsky speak at bookstores after work. If at any point they let slip that they had gone to prep school, or that their fathers were doctors or judges, I made a mental note to grade them harder when they spoke. As for the boys, their fathers were doctors and judges, too, and they also went to prep school, but they tried very hard to keep this a secret from me. Evo Morales had been elected Bolivia's first indigenous head of state and they were little baby Marxists. There was so much for us to bond over.

A few weeks into the internship, Jim called me into his office.

"Come in, Catalina. Close the door," he said.

I'd heard of performance reviews.

"Is this a performance review?" I asked.

"What? No. You're an intern. You're not in trouble. How old are you?"

"I'm twenty."

"You're a child."

I smiled.

"What do you call this?" he asked in a conspicuously neutral tone of voice, pointing to his lapel.

"That's your lapel?" I offered.

"Lah-pell," he said.

"Ah," I said, my face getting hot. I had pronounced it to rhyme with *apple*.

"Catalina, are you self-educated?" he asked. "Sometimes, you can tell when someone's self-educated because they have read all the books but they haven't heard the authors' names pronounced."

"Extremely not," I said. "I go to Harvard. That's the opposite of self-educated."

"Say this—G-o-e-t—h-e."

"I don't know. Didn't he write *Candide*? I loved *Candide*."

"No, that's Voltaire," he said. "Pronounce it for me?"

"I know who you're talking about but I don't know how to say it so I'm not going to try."

"There are idiosyncrasies to places like this," he said, taking a large breath before he began, primed as he was for his own long-windedness, "little rules that govern people's thinking and behavior. It's a code of the New York intellectual class, which is, unfortunately, where we find ourselves. Did I tell you where I grew up?" He had not. Jim Young was raised by a single mom in a trailer in rural Wisconsin. As a little boy, he was obsessed with *Moby-Dick*. In high school, it was Faulkner and *Absalom Absalom*. He was the first in his family to go to college—also Harvard, also on scholarship. During his junior year, while posting flyers for *The Advocate*, he told me, he was heard pronouncing "Nabokov" like how Sting says it in the Police song "Don't Stand So Close to Me." NAH-bah-kov. It outed him. Coetzee, Barthelme, those were tells. That he was not one of them.

Why hasn't anyone ever corrected me?

It's tricky, he explained. You don't want to be the kind of person who corrects someone's pronunciation, it would be uncomfortable for anyone, and here the racial dimension complicated the question in a very violent way. Besides, he thought there was a kind of condescension in it, a subconscious need to always have an outsider among them to remind them what they were not.

"The last thing I'll say, and then I promise I'll drop the dad thing—if you go to the parties, leave before the cocaine comes out."

I did not know if this was said seriously or in jest.

"I've never even ordered a drink," I said. Technically true. I was just shy of twenty-one, and though I drank what I believed to be untraceable amounts of hard liquor from the bottles my grandfather kept in the freezer and under the kitchen sink, I was afraid of breaking the law.

"Really? Don't you have a fake ID?"

"No, I don't," I said.

"Hmm," he said. "Please shut the door all the way on your way out. If I turn off the lights they won't know I'm here."

What Jim Young didn't understand was that I really was the opposite of self-taught. Even before Harvard, my education was supplemented by my grandfather's rousing post-dinner orations, back when I was small and willing to listen, and when he was younger and thrilled to be my guide. *Tonight, I will tell you about Rosalía Arteaga, Ecuador's first and only woman president,* he would say. *Tonight I'm going to explain the Great Colombia. Tonight you will learn about circumcision and the soccer fields Pablo Escobar built for the poor in Moravia. Tonight I will explain Sicilians.* He loved books but hated novels, dismissing the form entirely as girlish and indulgent. Gabriel García Márquez found his way inside our home on account of his duplicitousness, apparent ever since he was a young journalist who wanted to write a story about a shipwreck but found it would make a better story if he made it up. He was still a working journalist when his short stories were published in the newspaper. The first Gabo book my grandfather bought for me, off a street vendor in Jackson Heights, when I was around thirteen, was *News of a Kidnapping,* a semi-fictionalized account of a handful of high-profile cartel kidnappings in Colombia in the early '90s. I loved it.

I sometimes fear that everything I think and believe myself to feel about the world is just an amalgamation of passages from books I read as a kid or sound bites from opinions my grandfather expressed in 2004. The first time I saw a red toadstool mushroom, I felt like I should ask it for an autograph. I'd seen it drawn in storybooks time and again! It isn't always as nice as that, though. When I drink a Diet Coke, my brain immediately goes to my grandfather's lectures and I think, *Oh my god, Coca-Cola of Coca-Cola and the death squads.*

"Tell me again about the disappeared," I'd ask my grandfather. Los desaparecidos.

"Which ones?" he asked.

I could have just about died. Which ones? Which ones?!? He knew them all. The legendary Argentines. Of course the Chileans. The Colombians. The Haitians. The Peruvians. The Ecuadorians. I couldn't believe it. It's true, it's really true, Latin America was real.

My grandfather was a watchful man. "I have the eyes of an eagle, look," he'd say, pulling at a pale lower eyelid. He noticed on the subway, for example, that the kind of gringo who reads the *New York Post* was different from the kind of gringo who reads *The New York Times,* he couldn't quite put his finger on it, but the difference was obvious to him. He could understand the English of the *Daily News,* but he could not understand the English of *The New York Times,* and thus I would have to learn the English of *The New York Times.* He sent a money order and got me a subscription.

In early August before the start of my freshman year of high school, my grandfather taught me how to take the subway to school by practicing the route together. He timed me on his chunky black Casio, making us get out at random stops to test my ability to get back home or to school with that rerouting element thrown in. During "training," he made me wear a puffer coat to add a realistic yet extremely stressful element, because, he said, when you are running late—he knew I would be running late— and you are rerouted, and the trains are crowded, you'll be sweating out of pure rage.

My grandfather taught me how to pick a lock with two bobby pins; he taught me the extradition laws of major Latin American countries and France, Germany, and Switzerland; he taught me the difference between the Marxism of the Sandinistas and the FARC and how to make a Nescafé taste good (cinnamon and condensed milk). He said it was simply what you had to know as a cultured person, and that it was a shame that schools didn't teach anything these days.

I also knew from my grandfather that men might find me attractive. He started appraising me when I was little. He told me that I had a beautiful mouth but that I would look better if I stopped dressing like a callejera, which means streetwalker or hoodlum, depending. If he was in a good mood, he broke into dance and brought me into an embrace that became a silent cumbia or salsa or bachata or merengue. Even in the absence of music, pan-Latin pride had turned my body into a jukebox of tropical glossolalia. If my grandmother saw me in shorts or if a dress rode up and I didn't fix it, if I liked it, if I pulled it up to the tops of my thighs where they were prettiest, legs marquise cut on the table, she scolded me and arrived with a sweater or blanket, saying I needed to dress more modestly around my grandfather because even grandfathers are men. I might hear my grandfather walk around like a half-dead man in the middle of the night, fumbling for Nicorette lozenges in the kitchen drawers. When he went back to bed, he had to walk through my room—it was a railroad apartment—and he kissed me on the head thinking I was asleep. His hair was thick and black and it smelled faintly of pomade. He said that, too, that even grandfathers are men.

I very badly wanted to fall in love before graduating college. I had never been in love and being in love meant cues about how to feel and when. When I got dressed, I could look at myself how I imagined a boy in love might. I could see how, in the right lighting, even my headaches and nosebleeds, my sensitivity to light, the way I flinched at the slightest graze on my arm from a stranger, could be hot. A little eyeliner and a push-up bra and I could be one of Almodóvar's women on the verge of a nervous breakdown. But, for that, I'd need an audience. Lucky for me, boys constituted a reliable one.

I liked boys who smelled good and boys who couldn't drive. I liked boys who played soccer, and football, and baseball, and basketball, and tennis. I generally liked drummers. I liked sad Baptist boys from the south and tortured evangelicals from Hawaii. I liked boys who looked like a Harlem night in late July, positing the impossible, an eternal summer. I liked boys who leaned against walls, like Jordan Catalano, and boys who read DeLillo in the dining hall. I liked well-adjusted boys who were not hugged by their fathers and soulless boys with really cool moms. It didn't matter who they were. It mattered who I was. The character directions were clear, there were a few ways this could go, it was typecasting, but I could improvise here and there, make the part my own. I could do Natalie Portman in *Garden State* imagined as a cutter with a tan and borderline personality disorder, or Freida Pinto from *Slumdog Millionaire* with a nipple piercing and a Kafka tattoo. The same line would work on all of them. *I can be devastating in bed.*

It's a hard line to pull off, but I could be alright at it. I was never beautiful, exactly, but my body listened to me when I aimed it at men. I know that's how men write women, but how men write women is how I learned to speak English.

It was summer in New York and it is only in the summer that I look the way I imagine the Lord created me to look. Camilo was cute. Talking to him didn't feel like tennis. He would never take a risk. But I liked his arms and how I imagined I might feel in them. I didn't want regular sustenance and he wasn't offering, but then one day he asked for my phone number over office email because, I guess, the walk to my work station was prohibitive. He texted me immediately. *Hola, it's Camilo.*

I had found Camilo and life was now exciting. I would need new clothes, a new hair color, a deep conditioning treatment, new nails, I needed to exfoliate and shave and wax, I needed to do my eyebrows and think deeply and responsibly about bangs and whether I ever really gave bluegrass an honest try. I needed to decide what my trademark drink was, writers liked whiskey, but when I wanted to drink without my grandparents noticing I just poured a little of my grandfather's vodka into my Dr Pepper, which already has a medicinal smell, and Carrie Fisher drank Coke, Britney Spears drank Pepsi, Sprite has hood cred, but Dr Pepper has no bearing on the culture. Consider, too, whether "Catalina" needed a nickname. Would people call me Kitty? Katherine Kennedy went by Kick. How does one become a Kennedy? I felt like a young Joseph Kennedy, the grandson of Irish immigrants who wanted it all. But I wanted to *stay* a bootlegger, and also become president and attorney general and be Marilyn Monroe, too.

It was Camilo who introduced me to Lou Reed.

I'm struggling with how to phrase this. I was a girl for whom the gifting of a mixtape did not elicit surprise or, at this point, emotion. So when Camilo came by my desk and presented me

with a jewel-blue CD case labeled *Lou Reed for CMI* (my middle
name is Marisé), I was caught off guard by the sincerity of the
gesture. It didn't seem right that a smart boy would be so stunningly sincere. I stammered thanks.

He came by my desk every morning for three mornings straight
to ask if I'd listened to it yet. I hadn't had the time. On the fourth
morning, he told me I was going to take a little trip with him during our lunch break. The magazine was working summer hours,
which meant often nobody was in the office except the interns
and the receptionist.

At twelve noon, he came by my desk.

"Ready to go?"

"Am I allowed to know where we're going?"

"We'll just get off when we get off. Don't worry about it."

We walked to the Christopher Street subway station and took
the 1 Uptown.

Without saying anything to me, he took tangled headphones
out of his backpack, placed one earbud in his ear, handed me the
other earbud for my right year, and pressed Play.

We traveled twenty-five minutes uptown, which is roughly the
length it took to get through the Lou Reed playlist on his iPod.
"Sweet Jane." "Walk on the Wild Side." "Heroin." We got out only
to switch directions and headed back downtown to the office.

In the '70s, Lou Reed met a girl named Rachel Humphreys at
a nightclub in Greenwich Village. He was starstruck. She had not
been born *Rachel* and she had not been born *Humphreys*. Like
him, she was self-created, born a Mexican American child with
high cheekbones and full lips and jet-black hair. She was a trans
woman who worked as a drag queen. They began dating. The title
track on his 1975 record *Coney Island Baby* gives her a cute
shoutout—*I'd like to send this one out to Lou and Rachel, and all
the kids at P.S. 192!* Rachel came home bleeding one night. She

had been jumped. Keith Richards's doctor checked her over and said she was fine. Reed then called Andy Warhol for advice, who urged him to take her to the hospital. I don't know what happened next. In his diary, Warhol ends the anecdote by explaining he calls Rachel *she* but Reed misgenders her. It isn't quite a criticism. Then Rachel disappears from the books. She died young in 1990 of AIDS complications and was buried at Hart Island, a mass burial site off the coast of the Bronx where another million unclaimed bodies are buried, a pauper's grave.

The first thing the Europeans did when they stepped foot in the New World was name things. I, too, wanted to be discovered and named. I wanted everything wild in me to be given stupid little names like *Dendropsophus ozzy* and *elk*. In García Márquez, people in love experienced bouts of vomiting, psychosomatic fevers, and real catatonia. I wanted to make boys sick, too. This is how I wanted to be loved.

The only person in the world who really understood how to love me lived in Bushwick. Saint Bridget's was the local Puerto Rican–Ukrainian–Filipino church, the most pagan of the Catholic churches in the area. There was a six-foot statue of Jesus on the cross to the right of the altar. I wasn't Catholic anymore, but when I walked by, I felt an awful urge to go inside. Jesus lived there, and my love language was bloody sacrifice.

My grandmother said Jesus was created in the Lord's image and God was perfect so Jesus was the most perfect man to ever have existed and she and her friends in the congregation liked to talk about which handsome Hollywood man they thought Jesus probably looked like. The consensus at the time was Benicio del Toro with a beard.

I was baptized Catholic and had a First Communion. I went to Catholic school until the eighth grade and to Mass on Saturday nights. I looked forward to the homily most of all. I loved learning about Jesus. His best friend was John, and maybe they were in love, and he was also in love with Mary Magdalene, who was a prostitute, and when somebody touched him in a crowd he felt the energy leave his body. Taking Communion was a transcendent experience beyond what I'd thought possible. I accepted the host in my hands and as I walked back to my pew, the wafer entirely stuck to the roof of my mouth, I teared up at the thought that I was loved so much by this beautiful carpenter that he would prove it to me by slowly dying in front of me, his boys by his side, three sweet-talking felons bleeding out like John Leguizamo in the Baz Lurhmann movie. Best of all, he timed his death perfectly: He died young but not at the age of dorm room poster cliché. He was locked in at thirty-three, the age J.Lo was when she filmed "Jenny from the Block," young forever thanks to their pretty brown skin. Let's play nice with the other kids and volunteer a food metaphor to describe it. It was like the first bite into a charred marshmallow. It really was, is the thing.

Then when I was ten years old my grandparents announced we were becoming Jehovah's Witnesses. They no longer wanted the blood and gore of the Catholic Church. They wanted the fluorescent lights and dark blue carpeting of the Kingdom Hall, the lack of idols, the lack of images or art of any kind, and the books, all the books. My grandmother stopped watching soap operas and began dressing modestly, longer skirts, no red lipstick, pantyhose. It was a surprising change to see in someone so opposed to docility. I missed the Catholic Church. It was like going from wearing gold to wearing sterling silver.

Opportunities for leadership and service in the congregation were called "privileges" and the brothers and sisters who were given "privileges" were considered to be the most pious. When I was sixteen, an elder called my grandfather into the office where they had meetings with people who had been naughty. He read aloud a letter from headquarters stripping my grandfather of any honors and duties he had in the congregation, relieving him of his responsibilities as an usher and leader of congregation prayer. Anything that could be construed as a privilege was revoked. My grandfather was undocumented, the letter argued, so he was legally considered a *fugitive*. Christians needed to be model citizens, Jesus himself instructed his followers to render unto Caesar the things that are Caesar's, and fugitives did not. My grandfather left that room and he cried. This part I'm imagining. He would never tell me that. I'm imagining he cried.

Even at the Met, it was the rooms of medieval art that lit a fire in my heart. I thought about which of the relics in the room, the crucifixes and stained glass, might have survived the Spanish Inquisition. They had gold-plated crucifixes from 1125, from 1220, 1370, from 1450; a few of them were from the fifteenth century and sixteenth century. What if these were the exact crucifixes seen by my indigenous ancestors as their god king died? Had my African ancestors, brought to Latin America as slaves, seen this very crucifix during their forced conversions? And then my *other* ancestors, the white ones. Was there anything from the year Francisco Pizarro stepped foot in South America? I've seen two objects from 1532 at the museum and they are both boring. One is a nondescript silver gilded chalice from France, and the other is a round piece of stained glass that depicts the temptation of Saint Anthony, a holy man who renounced all human possessions and bodily desires for God and retired to the desert to live as a hermit; however, at night he had hallucinations of beasts and demons torturing him, for he could not escape temptation. Obviously German.

The stories of the Catholic martyrs were as real to me as the stories in the Old Testament, which were as real to me as the stories my grandfather told me about Ecuador and the stories my grandmother told me about herself. Which is to say, untrust-worthy. While my grandfather relived his time in military school with agonizing detail what felt like every night at the dinner table, I knew very little about my grandmother's life before America outside of what I have meagerly outlined for you here. My grand-mother had changing explanations for her glass eye. Tuberculo-sis, malaria, illnesses I could not really imagine resulting in a glass eye. Once, she told me that when she was very small, her birth mother struck her with a metal pail across the face, injuring her eye. She was never taken to the hospital. Shortly after that, just like me, she went to live with an aunt and uncle. It's unclear whether she was given away or taken away. I heard this story once and my grandmother never brought it up again. I knew to trea-sure this scrap of information and to not inquire further.

You can kill things by asking about them, but not by thinking about them.

It rained a lot in August. I made a habit of arriving home en-tirely drenched because I could never remember to pack an um-brella. Also, I liked the drama. Walking in the rain made me feel invisible, and for a long time I was. It could be horrifying, the way white people walked into me if I didn't move out of the way first, but other times being invisible was exhilarating. I could move through the city like no one could see me. I could be everywhere, all the time, and no one had to know. The city kept my secrets. When I finally made it home, and after I showered, I took my position on the floor at the foot of my grandma's love seat. I lay on my back and read while she watched *El Gordo y la Flaca.* I asked her if she had ever read *One Hundred Years of Solitude.*

"I won a writing contest on Gabriel García Márquez. Ah, you thought your old grandmother was a backwoods brute. I won first place in the whole school before you were even a gleam in your mother's eye!"

"What book was it, and did you actually read it?"

"It was *One Hundred Years of Ch—*, no it was . . . *Love in the Time of Cholera.*"

"You did not read that."

"I did so read it."

"What is it about?"

"Do you want me to tell you how I read it? Read one page, skip ten pages, read a page, skip ten pages, and so on and so forth. I felt like I understood the point. It's not that complicated, and besides, it was way too long."

It was easy to love my grandmother when she was like this. Silly, irreverent, self-aware.

"Now run down to the bodega, Milagrito, and pick up my lotto ticket."

My little miracle.

Every Friday, my grandmother asked me to stop by the bodega and pick up a lotto ticket and every Friday she asked me to pick the numbers. I felt embarrassed by the sincerity of the request and quietly pointed at the most emotionally charged numbers I could think of—my birth date, her birth date, the birth dates of my dead parents.

Despite our conversion, my grandmother held on to old gods, old traditions, her own way of doing things. Take the lottery. The lottery was considered gambling, which was prohibited. But my grandfather thought I was lucky, and my grandmother was no fool. If her granddaughter was a rabbit's foot, she was going to put it to the test. She still believed in miracles, maybe because of me but mostly because of Elián González and the dolphins. Elián was five when he was lost at sea, the only survivor on the balsa he was floating on from Cuba. His mother drowned. My grandmother was one of the many people who believed he survived because dolphins surrounded his raft and protected him. Above my bed was a gold-framed Precious Moments poster depicting a blond ballerina with the text, "Lord, keep me on my toes." It took some effort to reach it. Hidden inside the frame was a stash of old lotto tickets folded in half, and two conspicuously maroon passports, mine and my grandmother's, a dream of escape for two undocumented gals.

Summer was nearing its end, and I was crestfallen. Nothing had *happened* to me. Nothing exciting, nothing definitive; no awakening of any kind. My thing with Camilo had stalled. My grandmother sensed my restlessness, and I saw how she tried to accommodate the slightest chance for adventure.

"You know what I was thinking?" she said one afternoon, from the couch. "If you want to stay out later with your Mexican friend, you should take a taxi home. I don't want you on the subway late." She handed me a twenty-dollar bill, so I wouldn't have to ask my grandfather.

"Mira, Catalina," she said in a low, grave voice. "You are never going to have to ask a man for money. You will never extend your hand and ask a man for a coffee, or a sanitary napkin, or a home. You have to promise me."

I promised.

My grandmother should have just kept her money. When I told Camilo that my grandfather wanted me home by 10:00 P.M. on weekdays, he didn't ask me to break my curfew for just one night like every single one of the outsiders from *The Outsiders* probably would have. He tried to *honor* it, checking his watch nervously like he wanted to impress my fucking grandfather, like bringing me home on time and not fucking me was going to impress my fucking grandfather. It made him look pitiful in my eyes. I could see in Camilo, at age twenty-one, even under the shadow cast by his devastating starman profile, that he had firm opinions about the kemptness of lawns, and how one should be treated by hotel staff on a trip to the Dominican Republic, Wallace Stevens walking to his executive job at an insurance company in Hartford every morning for decades, even after winning the Pulitzer, writing poems on the back of permission-slip-looking cop shit in Connecticut. I could have been on that path, too, but I don't look like Wallace Stevens, a curse at the root of all of my pleasures, and a factor in some of my great melancholies.

PART TWO
Fall Semester

ONE OF THE first things I observed at Harvard, days after moving in as a freshman, is that marveling at Annenberg, the freshman dining hall, made you seem like a tourist. It was indeed beautiful, if a little gauche, shaped like a cathedral, three stories tall, stained glass windows, huge chandeliers, marble plaques etched with names of Harvard men who died in various wars. But it was important not to act impressed. You can *be* impressed, I suppose, though *impressed* isn't the word I'd use for what I felt. I had learned long ago to make my eyes go dead in front of anything or anyone that commanded attention. It was a matter of dignity.

At my high school graduation, my tenth-grade Hotels and Hospitality teacher gave me some advice. "I want to give you some advice, Catalina," he said. "At this school, you were a big fish in a small pond. At Harvard, you will be a very small fish in a very big pond, and it is best to approach with humility." For my first three years at Harvard, I heeded that advice, kept my head down, and sir'd and ma'am'd my elders. This was another way to keep my dignity intact, avoiding perception and judgment, invisibility by design. By the start of senior year, I could tell in my bones that I was done. For three years, I had been too busy feeling small and tragic to accept my razzle-dazzle coming-of-age at the most famous school in the world. Things were different now. There was catching up to do. I felt like I was emerging whole and without a backstory, like Athena born from Zeus's forehead fully formed.

I was also sad and lonely. I had spent those first three years dumping my would-be friends for a variety of reasons: Brian showed me a thirteen-minute skateboarding video set to a Foo Fighters song, Victor made a sexist joke about Feist at the expense of Fiona Apple, I made out with Josephine's ex-boyfriend while they were on a break, that one's on me.

I had never been good at keeping friends and was especially perplexed by the riddle of female friendship. I imagined that girls didn't like me, which was why I was never invited to brunch, or birthday parties, or tailgates before football games, but the truth is that I was invited, I just didn't show up. I'd forget, fall ill, stand them up, be too embarrassed to talk to them again. Boys were easier on me when I did stuff like that. I could disappear for weeks or months at a time, and they didn't ask questions. Sometimes they didn't even notice.

Delphine Rodriguez was my closest friend at Harvard. Delphine was Puerto Rican with deep olive skin and freckles in small clusters around sparkly black eyes. I was usually self-conscious around other Latinas at school. I knew too much about them. Everything about me hurt, and I imagined that everything about them hurt, too, and in the exact same ways. I imagined their rain boots were, like mine, from TJ Maxx. That's why I listened to the Decemberists. But I wanted to be close with Delphine and I couldn't tell you why. I met her during a freshman year dorm

icebreaker that she dominated. The RA, a first-year at the Harvard Divinity School studying to be an Episcopalian minister,
said, "When did you realize you were funny?" and Delphine said,
"When my mother killed herself." I was motherless, too. Delphine and I looked like two different characters from the same
cartoon animator. We had large, dark eyes and dark eyelids and
even darker under eyes, like drawings Tim Burton might have
discarded for looking too ethnic. Every Halloween I wanted us to
go as the creepy twins from the Diane Arbus photograph but
Halloween was a bridge too far for Delphine. Like me, Delphine
also grew up a Jehovah's Witness. We would have looked fucking
terrifying.

We became very close very quickly. Since becoming friends,
we'd gotten matching heart tattoos on our ankles, matching belly
piercings, a BFF necklace. What we had wasn't romantic, but it
was urgent and possessive and full of ups and downs. If we had
been married, we would have had so many vow renewals. Our
relationship suffered a blow sophomore year, the year of the historic 2008 election. Delphine was an American citizen, and she
did not vote. Jehovah's Witnesses were supposed to remain neutral in political affairs, a neutrality that included not voting, but I
was certain that if I was an American citizen, I would vote. I made
it my mission to get Delphine to register. I sent her links. I sent
her reminders. She did not register to vote, and she did not vote.
It felt personal. I didn't understand a ton about American elec-
toral politics aside from what Jon Stewart explained on *The Daily
Show* but I felt in my heart that people who were politically neutral were cowards.

Then, junior year, I decided to throw us a joint birthday party.
Neither of us grew up with birthdays because Witnesses don't do
that, either, so I went to Dollar Tree and bought fifty dollars'
worth of '90s toys that we didn't get as kids—a box of sixty-four

crayons, a Tamagotchi. She cried when she saw the gifts. Delphine pawed at a slice of ice cream cake as I complained that neither of my grandparents had called to acknowledge my birthday.

"At least you have parents," Delphine snapped.

I paused for a long time.

"Well, they're not my parents."

"That's a technicality."

"It's not really a technicality."

"Okay? They raised you since you were little, they're basically your parents. You're always together all the time, you do everything together, it's like the Brady Bunch."

"My parents are fucking *dead*, Delphine."

Delphine rarely lashed out, but I admit I had been pushing and pushing with the voting, the birthday party, and the Halloween costume planning. Unlike me, Delphine still went to meetings, though only on Sundays. When I moved to Cambridge, it was my grandparents' expectation that I join the local congregation. Copy and paste myself from Queens into Cambridge. I tried. I went to the Kingdom Hall and challenged myself to say hello to one person before I sprinted for the exit. As soon as I said I was new to the area because I was a student, they looked at me differently. Young people attending this particular Kingdom Hall were in town to study at Harvard and MIT. The elders saw us as ticking time bombs about to start believing in evolution and going to Halloween parties. And they were right! At least for me. Delphine had one foot out and one foot in.

I started out senior year agnostic and in a little bit of a pickle. There was an outstanding balance on my tuition bill. I had a full scholarship, but I still needed to make a contribution toward my education, something of a symbolic gesture, and I had no way of paying for it, symbolic or not. The financial aid officers could not encourage me to seek out work because that was illegal and I could not ask my grandparents for money, because they had none, and without a social security number I didn't qualify for a bank loan so the Harvard Financial Aid Office offered me a personal loan. I agreed to pay them back over the next ten years and also to give back to the community by volunteering at one of the Harvard institutions that are open to the public.

I was assigned to the Peabody Museum of Archaeology and Ethnology. The Peabody was an old redbrick building on a dead-end tree-lined street called Divinity Avenue. It was bookended by cherry blossom trees that bloomed most obnoxiously every spring. It didn't feel like a museum. It felt like someone's Connecticut mansion that happened to have on display a bear claw necklace acquired by Lewis and Clark along with Andean textiles and Incan metalwork adorning the walls. The initial money to build it was put up by its namesake, George Peabody, a rags-to-riches Massachusetts financier who wanted to make good on his success by promoting arts and culture. And promote culture he did, kind of! For example, a lot of the museum's South America collection came from a Swiss biologist who believed that Black people were a physiologically and anatomically distinct species.

Thanks to these great men, I could now give back to the Harvard community. It felt like a plum job. I wasn't getting paid, but I was surrounded by beauty and air-conditioning and helpful guidelines about appropriate behavior. I knew not to bring in my backpack and to stand six feet away from paintings. Plus, museum security guards are the least coppish of all cops. Out of all security and law enforcement officers in the world, I think the nicest ones are the guards at the Met.

I was working at the museum front desk one splendid sunny

morning a few weeks into the semester when I received an email from the David Rockefeller Center for Latin American Studies, or DRCLAS, which we pronounced "Doctor Klass."

Dear Catalina:

Congratulations! Your junior essay, *Magical Realism and Narcoliterature,* has been selected for the William Yandell Elliott Prize. Please join us at our Fall Reception for refreshments, cocktails, and congratulations. The William Yandell Elliott Prize comes with an award of $500, which will be awarded at the reception.

I smiled. I liked prize money almost as much as I liked standardized tests, which was a lot. I looked up William Yandell Elliott to see just how prestigious the award was and learned he was a mentor to Henry Kissinger, my favorite Harvard alum. Even better.

Thanks to my grandfather, I can't remember a time when I didn't know about Henry Kissinger, like how I can't place when I first heard James Earl Jones's voice as Darth Vader. I knew he was responsible for the illegal bombing of Cambodia during the Vietnam War, I knew he had some sort of deal with the military dictatorships of Argentina and Chile. What was he doing these days? Consulting, probably.

Mr. Kissinger deserved to be punished. Don't you think? Sometimes I imagined him in a storage container by the highway inside my brain. He'd get a latrine, a really high-tech latrine that empties itself and that I do not have to set up or fiddle with. Dr. Kissinger would obviously get a comfortable bed. I am not here to torture. I am not here to inflict pain. His meals will be provided in the form of a pill. We want him to stay alive because he is here to generate power. There is no way for him to escape me. He just has to be a good boy and do his job.

Actually, this container contains many little Henry Kissingers. One is not enough. I have condemned them all to running on a treadmill to generate power for my little body, and we use that power for things like flirting, which men and women from around the globe have delighted in for years, and other things that I dutifully perform like my grit, resilience, and Protestant work ethic. The Henry Kissingers power my body. They are very good at running on treadmills and getting me to parties.

My grandmother loved it when I went to parties. She didn't like my drinking—she wasn't dumb and she worked hard to wash the wine-stained interior of my green Nalgene bottle whenever I was home on break—but she liked it when I went to parties because she could help me plan what to wear. After reading the invitation from DRCLAS, I abandoned the desk and ran across the narrow street to call her, nearly knocking over a boy smoking a cigarette on the museum's front steps. I crouched behind a bus stop alcove to avoid being spotted by anyone who might have had opinions about my whereabouts. I glanced back as the phone rang.

"Abuela, guess what? No, really, guess what?"

"What?"

"Oh, there is a cute boy across the street."

"What does he look like?"

"He has curly dark hair like the guy from RBD."

"Which one?"

"The cute one with curly black hair."

"Ah ah ah, que nice. Guapo."

My grandmother never told me to marry a white person to "better our race." I've heard it said before by other grandmothers, just not mine. Marriage was never in her plans for me. Neither were children. She never had a hurt, perverse fantasy about the racial mixture of my children because I was not going to have children.

"Catalina, is that what you are calling to tell me?" she asked, pretending to be annoyed.

"I won a writing prize and there's going to be a reception and I have absolutely nothing to wear. I'm going to die."

"You won't die."

"Yes, I will die. If I don't find something to wear I will wilt away like a rose, petal by petal, J.Lo as Selena in *Selena,* releasing the diamond ring inside her hand as she dies."

The boy I had noticed was still across the street, back by the Peabody entrance. He was taller than I was by a lot but I don't believe he was especially tall. He smiled a little, and I thought it was possible he was looking at me.

My grandmother laughed.

"Nooo, you won't die."

"I will definitely die."

"I'll find you a dress and then you won't die."

I stood up and walked back to the Peabody.

"Okay, pedazo de tonta, I have to go back to work. I'm sneaking back in now. Bendición," I said as I approached the steps.

The boy, now only feet away, was looking straight at me.

I hung up.

"What did your mother say?" he said, putting out his cigarette under the toes of his Nikes.

"What makes you think it was my mother?"

"How you spoke to her just now, it had to be an older person and I don't see you cursing out your grandma."

I could tell he wanted me to be impressed. He wanted me to ask him how he knew Spanish, but I was not curious because there were a finite number of explanations for a boy such as him at a place such as this and I felt no interest in exploring the known world.

"My mother is dead," I said.

What a line. He scanned my eyes to see if I was serious.

"Nathaniel," he said, and stuck out his hand. "You're Catalina, right?"

"We've met?"

"Phil Fisher's postwar American Lit class freshman year," he said. "We were in the same section. But it's cool. It was a big section."

"Oh. Yeah." Now I remembered him. He hated Flannery O'Connor.

"Could you tie my shoe?" I said suddenly, my voice breaking slightly. I cleared my throat. "I don't think I can kneel in this dress. It's too short."

I had impulsively cut off the bottom ten inches of my dress before running to the museum that morning. I was hot all the time, and I go bananas when I sweat, so I wore flimsy floral dresses from Forever 21, Target, or H&M. My scissors were dull and the results revealed a dress way shorter in the back than in the front, but the feeling of the fabric on my calves had been too much to bear.

Nathaniel widened his eyes but knelt anyway.

"So you just say things, sometimes?" he asked, tying the laces on my white leather Oxfords, shoes my grandmother bought specifically so I could wear them to parties with boys. "Like, you say whatever you want? Because it amuses you?"

His words were angry but his face was wild with happy things in it. I smiled and walked into the building. Nathaniel followed me inside. We took our respective positions. Me behind the desk, him in front of it, leaning forward in his dark blue jeans and black T-shirt. He signed in to work with one of the collections under the supervision of the anthropologist and head conservator, Dr. Murphy, whose office was on the second floor. I printed out a pass for him.

"*Nathaniel Wheeler*," I read. "What are you, an archaeologist?"

"I'm in Anthropology," he said. "And you're in, let me guess, Folk and Myth?"

Folklore and Mythology was a real major. It was a campus joke. But it was also a source of pride. How much more liberal-arts-college could you get?

"*Ha ha,*" I said in a deadpan. "No. English."

"That would have been my second guess," he said.

"Are you sure you're not in Art History?" I returned.

At Harvard, it was usually white girls with money who studied Art History, daughters of war criminals, heiresses to fortunes made in something dirty like railroads or sugar.

A school group came in.

"I guess I'll see you around," he said.

"No," I said. "Stay."

"Me?" he asked, unnecessarily.

"I'm bored and you're not boring."

Nathaniel stepped to the side of the table, closer to me, while the schoolteachers counted their kids. I felt him looking at me, so I tried to appear as wholesome as possible, like Mary on that holy night.

"You're very good at this," he said.

"What am I good at?"

"Flirting effectively."

"Effectively! Wow. What do you think my goal is?"

"I'm not sure," he said. "But I never turn down a challenge."

"That is a very aggressive thing to say."

He said, "I gotta go, Catalina," and then he was gone. I wanted to watch him go, to see if he looked over his shoulder like in the movies. But the sea of schoolchildren drowned him out.

✳ •

In the fall of our junior year, my friend Kyle Johnson nominated me for the Signet, an arts and letters secret society so secret that it had a website with the names of members going back one hundred years. Kyle was Black and Jewish. *Like Drake,* I said. *Yes, like Drake,* he said. He was not popular in the traditional sense but he was the editor in chief of *The Crimson,* and people trusted his opinions. He read the right books, liked the right movies. And he liked me.

Kyle was a writer and had been a member of the Signet since his sophomore year. The expectation was that members be successful in their art in the world outside of Harvard. Some members were touring violinists or opera singers. Others were actors who filmed movies on summers off from school. Like almost everywhere else on campus you had to audition, or "comp," to get into the Signet, but before you could comp, you had to be nominated by someone who was already a member, which kept that world small and white. Kyle nominated me because he thought I was a good writer and he liked that I dressed like Erin Brockovich. But it was also his way of sticking it to the artsy kids at Harvard. He worked alongside them, and he was friends with them, but that's not where his loyalties lay. He nominated me to remind them of that.

You can't pretend you don't give a shit when you're comping a secret society. You clearly care, a lot. The thing about being at Harvard is that in order to be there at all, you would have had to be the kind of person who *applies* to Harvard. You weren't necessarily a megalomaniac if you went to Harvard, but it helped if you were. I was no different than the others but I still only attended one out of the three required social events involved in comping the Signet.

"They like your vibe," he said.

"The not-showing-up-to-things vibe?"

"They think you're urbane," he shrugged. "That you don't care what other people think."

I accepted that reading with relief, happy to be misread, happy to be thought of at all.

Kyle and I first met in a poetry seminar freshman year. We sat across the table from each other, and we were friendly, we said hi and hello, but on the day the class discussed the famous fascist and anti-Semite poet Ezra Pound, Kyle left his copy of *Cantos* untouched, unopened, in front of him on the table, the spine not remotely cracked, the receipt hanging out. He smiled cheerfully throughout his protest. I waited for him after class.

"I saw what you did, with the book and the uncracked spine. I thought that was cool."

"Oh, that?"

"It's the only thing I'll ever remember about *Cantos*."

Kyle smiled and reached for my hand. "Do you have anywhere to be right now?"

Also, Kyle was gay. With sex off the table, anything was possible. It allowed for an intimacy that was gushing and free. I felt relaxed around him. I dropped my shoulders, and the tightness in my stomach disappeared. I let him link his arm with mine when we walked down the cobblestoned streets and leaned on his shoulder when I was sleepy. I wouldn't know Boston outside of Irish sports bars at all if it weren't for Kyle. He loved coffee, and he was always asking me to go into Boston with him to do our work in this or that new coffee shop. His order was a triple iced Americano.

Kyle was the first classmate at Harvard I told I was undocumented, even before Delphine. It was a different time. The Pulitzer Prize–winning journalist Jose Antonio Vargas would not publicly come out as undocumented on the cover of *The New York Times Magazine* for three more years. Once, in high school, I briefly mentioned not having a social security number in a paper and my teacher asked me to stay after class where he told me I needed to be more discreet and discerning in who I entrusted with potentially endangering information. I thought of this when an undocumented Harvard sophomore was detained at a Texas airport for trying to board a plane with only his Harvard ID at the end of summer break.

In the middle of a sleepless night only a few weeks into our friendship, I sent Kyle an email.

To: Kyle Johnson
From: Catalina Ituralde
Subject: A Big Thing
2:47 A.M. EST

It's very funny I am telling you this at the beginning of our friendship and not somewhere in the middle or simply not at all. Harvard is aware, and the Deans are all aware, Sofia Vergara and Gloria Estefan must be personally aware, but I was born in South America and my visa expired when I was a kid and 9/11 complicated things to such an incredible degree there is no way to get it un-expired. Literally not a single way. Harvard got me a visit with the best immigration lawyer in New England who works with kids in my situation, he talked to me pro bono and basically he said: marriage or legislation. So literally not a single way. Anyway, I hope your political persuasions parallel mine in some way and you aren't politically disturbed by this. You can

be—and in that case, we would not work out as friends probably. It doesn't really . . . come up as an issue ever. Except logisti-
cally, sometimes. But not usually.—Catalina

Kyle responded quickly.

From: Kyle Johnson
To: Catalina Ituralde
Subject: Re: A Big Thing
5:30 A.M. EST

I love your email, you're amazing, and, no, I'm not some whack-
a-doo Log Cabin Republican who doesn't want to be your friend.
If anything, should you become the face of immigration reform,
I'm all about playing stoic and/or weepy best friend who gives
an impassioned speech in your defense before the glaring lights
of the news cameras. Not that I'm a fame whore or anything.
Go to sleep.

When I got into the Signet, I was given a key to a little blue
cottage at 46 Dunster Street. The clubhouse awning bore a gilded
bee. Members were Drones, and we signed emails with *bzzzz*.

The Signet clubhouse hosted lunch every day of the week. It
was really nice food. Homemade pomegranate bread, always
served warm and with butter, braised chicken with artichoke
hearts, warm brie, apple cider and sparkling water, squash soup
and pear and endive salad and soufflés and raspberry tarts. You
were allowed to invite one person to lunch with you, ideally an
interesting and illustrious adult, preferably an alumnus. There
was at least one alumnus at every lunch. Alumni appreciated my
presence. I was proof incarnate that their generous donations to

Harvard were being put to good use, proof incarnate that Harvard was keeping up with the times. They also loved my company. When they asked, I told them I wanted to be a writer. *Everything is copy*. I loved that. I quoted it to old white ladies with jade brooches who appreciated Nora Ephron and were thrilled to look at me and see themselves.

Ms. Lily Rose Brinckerhoff was European of some kind, her accent was untraceable. She came to lunch every Wednesday dressed in head-to-toe Eileen Fisher. We bonded over our hatred of Uggs.

"Uggs are the rock bottom of American girlhood," she said.

"Exactly," I said.

I could not afford Uggs, and I hated their ubiquity. I do not know which of these came first.

We were both wearing hats. She was wearing a beige wool beret and brown cashmere turtleneck. I was wearing a leopard wide-brimmed hat.

"Why don't people wear hats anymore?" she asked me. "Is there no more fun?"

"And Patagonia fleeces." I shuddered. "I would rather die than announce to the world I've given up, a.k.a. I'd rather die than wear Patagonia." I could, incidentally, also not afford Patagonia.

Then, one day, it happened.

"Look at this gorgeous complexion," she said while she softly touched my bare arm. I flinched. "Are you Spanish, my dear?"

Not this, no.

"I am Latina, yeah. I speak Spanish."

"What is your background?"

"My family is from Ecuador, but I've been in America since I was five. I'm from Queens."

"Before I retired, I used to have an assistant, and she was Ecuadorian, too. Let me tell you, she was one of the kindest, hardest-working, honest-to-god good women and she had a really hard life. 'Oh Lily Rose,' she would cry to me, 'life is so unfair.' She was such a good woman. Rosario Suarez?"

"I don't know her," I said blankly.

"Do you visit Ecuador often?"

"No," I said. "My grandparents came here for a reason and I think they want to look forward and not back."

She looked at me with an extended sympathetic smile.

"One day, though," I sighed, remembering my lines. "Maybe one day I'll visit the homeland."

"Well, why don't you? Traveling is one of the best things a young person can do. Nobody ever regrets it. Go out, see the world, take a couple of years off after you graduate and visit the rainforest. Oh, if I was your age, the trouble I'd get myself into!"

White people have always tried to bond with me about Latin America in this anxious, insecure, and very awkward way. I never had anything to contribute to these conversations, which were largely based on vacations to Machu Picchu or Rio de Janeiro. I didn't know how to surf. I didn't know how to swim. I was terrified of South American animals. Vicuñas, toucans, anacondas, no. I did not know a thing about mosquito nets or the diarrhea and vertigo from altitude sickness. I did not know about hiking. I never had to acclimate myself to the elevation. I never had to climb up. One minute I did not exist on this Earth and the next I was wailing in the sky.

The one person I imagined someday asking to lunch at the Signet was Professor Ruby Sandoval. Professor Sandoval was Harvard's first Latina tenured professor and an absolute star on campus. Her hair was shiny, curly, and black. Her skin was a deep warm brown and she had the tiniest, sparkliest diamond in her nose. One of the most iconic things about Ruby Sandoval is that she wore leather pants, and often. Nothing about it was vulgar, they looked as demure as a pair of Anne Taylor slacks but they were decidedly not Anne Taylor slacks. She was a Latina with a full professorship and she wore perfectly tailored Italian leather pants. It said something. She wasn't here to lie low.

I was a lifelong teacher's pet and I expected to charm Professor Sandoval in her "Intro to Cultural Theory" seminar the way that I charmed all of my other teachers, but I could immediately see that she was not especially charmed by me. There were not many Latine faculty in my orbit, only two or three, and our connection made me scared of disappointing her. It felt like we were all somehow reflections of each other. I carried with me the vague notion that Professor Sandoval would one day have to defend me against the Harvard board who just needed a minute with me to realize I was a liability and a joke.

Harvard was my introduction to academic jargon and I struggled to keep up. I did not understand theory. I knew I was smart, and well-read, and if I did not understand what I was reading, I concluded, correctly, that most people would not be able to understand what I was reading, which made me indignant. What was bizarre to me was the realization the books were intentionally written that way. It fucked with my head. I fought everything Professor Sandoval taught. I fought Claude Lévi-Strauss and Clifford Geertz. I dismissed all of Marx and Engels. I scowled at Deleuze and Guatarri and rolled my eyes at Gloria Anzaldúa. I don't think Ruby Sandoval appreciated that. By the end of that first semester, it became clear we had nothing in common except, I guess, the most important thing.

Still, she was a good teacher. She was hard on us. It was nice to have someone be hard on me. In the cultural theory class I took with Sandoval, she carefully marked up my papers. Above a generalization I made about the Cuban American population in Miami she once wrote in purple ink: *NOOOOOOOOOOOOOOOOOOOOOOO*

I taped that page to my wall above my desk.

✳ •

What I sometimes dreamed of, in my most private, impossible dreams, hidden inside a vault, safe within a safe, was to be a boy reporter on the eve of a revolution. Men got to die quick, glorious deaths among and with each other. In every single war across the world, across history, across all time, I would have been a civilian and a girl, the victim of an inglorious death. I would have been one of the women and children drowning in third class on the *Titanic*. In America, how could I die? Ravaged by disease or injury and unable to pay for treatment? Killed by a run-of-the-mill man who felt slighted in an elevator? My body disposed of in a suitcase? It wasn't right.

By the time the Colombian journalist Abél Morrison set foot on campus, I'd clocked one hundred and eighty hours of daydreams about him. It had been a long road getting him to Harvard. His whistleblowing reporting—covering the false positives scandal in Colombia, wherein special forces killed young civilian men and dressed their corpses in guerrilla outfits to meet U.S.-backed quotas—had upset the Colombian president, and the American consulate in Bogotá said he was permanently banned from getting a visa under the Patriot Act. But when Harvard extended him a fellowship in which all he had to do was teach one undergraduate class, they didn't take the consulate's no for an answer and they didn't have to.

Abél Morrison had famously tried heroin with Hunter S. Thompson, the prophet of gonzo journalism. For Thompson,

Latin America was full of raw materials. Cocaine, violence,
women—inspiration. Abél didn't talk about it, but among the
Latin Americanists on campus it was lore. I was starstruck
when I heard that. There was no greater celebrity to me than
heroin.

Abél dressed exactly how you'd imagine a Latin American leftist would dress. Leather jacket; tight jeans; boots; messy, greasy
black hair; pierced ears; a resounding silence about his past. I
heard that in his youth he was involved in guerrilla activity of
some kind. He didn't bring it up, so I didn't ask him, and I didn't
ask around. I believe people are allowed their secrets.

On Tuesdays and Thursdays, I took Abél's seminar "El Ejér-
cito, La Policía, y El Narco." On the first day of class, he passed
out blank maps of the United States and asked us to label all fifty
states plus Puerto Rico and identify which Mexican cartel controlled the local markets region by region. I got a D+.

Abél's class was one of a handful of courses I took at Harvard
devoted to the subject of my ancestry. I figured out quickly that
in order to learn about Latin America, I had to go to Anthropology or Literature. There were no professors of Latin American
History at Harvard. Real live Latin Americans taught in the Romance Languages and Literatures Department but the professors and TAs for most of my Anthro classes were white. Like
Darth Vader, Mickey Mouse, and Henry Kissinger, I have always known about anthropologists. Now I learned about Anthropology students. The boys wore stacks of woven bracelets
on their wrists. The girls had nose piercings. They were proud
when they drank a brown person under the table, proud they
could handle the hottest chile pepper. It was, of course, polite to
let them win.

Even Abél's class was housed in Anthropology. Walking through
the Anthro building on the way to class, I was able to tell who was

taking Anthropology 154: Intro to the Andes by the dreamy look in their eyes. I could tell who was taking Anthropology 399: Mesoamerica by the appearance of beaded earrings and peasant blouses where hoops and hoodies had been earlier. I had taken both classes as soon as I could. Inside the lecture halls, seeing Latines from all over was thrilling, even if I had little interest in befriending them. The Latines from Texas were not like the Latines from Alaska who were not like the Latines from Matamoros who were not like the Latines from the Bronx. It was a revelation. Maybe I had no idea where their rain boots came from. Telemundo had told us that Latines looked like Mexican-born Polish actresses for so long that I'd almost forgotten what we looked like, but here we were, everything at once. Whatever our cinematic personal fantasy was, we were almost all descendants of annihilated peoples. We wanted to learn about them, together. What did their clothes look like? What did they eat? Who were their gods?

My grandfather was a blowhard about Latin American political and military history. He was just one of those guys who doesn't shut up about the navy. Whenever I was home on a break, I brought up all the exciting new things I was learning in class and he supplemented my lectures with his own books, YouTube videos, disc jockey segments, and protest songs. My grandfather and Harvard anthropologists tag-teamed my education on the Americas and the truth is they agreed on the basic story. First came the Spaniards, and with them the Church, then came petroleum, then came cocaine, then came NAFTA, and now we were all fucked.

I wrote an essay for Abél on my memories of visiting poppy fields as a girl, memories I could not place. That happened a lot. I sometimes saw flashes of images, remembered snippets of dialogue—they could be nightmares, they could be memories, they could be Nestlé advertisements, but they were all in my head. The first sentence was: *While I have seen cocaine, I have never laid my eyes on coca, the sacred plant my ancestors used ceremoniously.*

"Fantastic work, I am impressed by your insistence on telling, not showing," Abél said as he passed the paper back to me at the end of class while students filed out the door. "You'll see I marked you down because the point of the paper was to use primary sources."

"You mean the point of the *essay*," I corrected him. "And *I* was my primary source."

"Sometimes I wish Uribe had just killed me," he said under his breath.

*

As soon as I saw the news on my Yahoo! home page, I sent Delphine an email.

My birthday has been ruined. I absolutely hate him.

The Nobel Prize in Literature had just been announced. Peruvian novelist Mario Vargas Llosa. We *hated* Mario Vargas Llosa. He was a neoliberal and increasingly a puppet of the West. She responded immediately.

I'm shocked, I thought this was Philip Roth's year. Also, happy birthday, babe.

I was rooting for Javier Marías. Not this travesty.

We need a crisis meeting, over LEGAL drinks.

Yes.

I met Delphine that night at the Playwright, a dark Irish bar with the Harvard logo everywhere that never carded. I was turning twenty-one, it's true, but still the only ID I had was my Ecuadorian passport and I did not enjoy taking it out to be inspected by bouncers with flashlights. Delphine glided in like a pretty Christian drone. She was wearing a white men's Brooks Brothers shirt with metallic black American Apparel leggings, thick white crew socks, and Birkenstocks. She wore her hair up, secured by gold pins. I only saw Delphine with her hair down a handful of times, and even then it only lasted for a few moments; her hair was so long and so thick and so heavy that it needed to be off her face. In those brief moments when I caught a glimpse of her, I felt like I was witnessing a miracle.

Even how she gave her drink order was a marvel. She ordered a gin and tonic, no preference for gin, house gin was fine. We were in college and the culture was *broke college student* independent of and notwithstanding any student's actual financial situation. Delphine was upper-middle-class, that elusive chanteuse. She was very, very loved by her father, Hector Rodriguez, who raised her as a single dad in Texas. He was a veteran. They lived around Mexican American families who did not always make them feel welcome. Mr. Rodriguez was Black. Not African American. Afro Latino. Delphine's mom had also been Puerto Rican, pink skin, pink cheeks, green eyes, curly dark hair. Together, they made Delphine, who primarily identified as Texan.

High school was hard for Delphine. She wasn't even asked to prom and she was the most beautiful girl at her school. Trust me. But small-town Texas didn't know what to do with her. Not the white kids. Not the Chicanos. Not the Black students. Not the newly arrived Mexicans. She looked . . . *mixed.* What, exactly, was she? To whom did she owe her life and her allegiances?

Mr. Rodriguez gave Delphine a Cartier *Love* bracelet for her high school graduation. It certainly looked the part at Harvard—that bracelet or some iteration of it was on every other wrist, it seemed like—but on Delphine it looked different. She wore it different. She looked like Robert Lowell clutching to his chest Lucian Freud's portrait of Lady Caroline Blackwood, at one point or another a lover of both, as he died of a heart attack in a cab. It was Art. Her thing, by the way, was organic chemistry. She was premed.

Delphine had an enormous workload, but she seemed to have a system worked out. When she really needed to hit the books she slept three hours, worked three hours, slept three hours, worked three hours. She swore it made her more efficient.

"My roommate keeps having incredibly loud creepy sex while I'm trying to study. I don't know if the sex itself is creepy, but it's creepy that they're so loud when they know I'm there!"

"Maybe you need to go out there and put a pep in your step yourself."

"Ew, Catalina!" she groaned. "Never, ever say that again."

"I have to tell you something," I said after the server brought out our drinks. "The other day outside of work this guy was looking at me and I asked him to tie my shoe, one because I really did need to tie my shoe without flashing everybody, and two because he was cute and I wanted to see if I could get him to do it and he was nonreactive. He did it, but he didn't, like, *react* to me in any particular way. I was like, *huh*," I said.

"Ooh. What's his name?"

"Nathaniel Wheeler. I'm sure I can get past the name."

She cocked her head with amusement. "Nathaniel Wheeler as in Byron Wheeler?"

"Who?" I said, trying in vain to use the red stirring stick as a straw, already halfway into my vodka soda.

"Byron Wheeler, the British director," she said. "That's his *dad*."

And then it clicked. Byron Wheeler. I read *Yahoo! Celebrity* fairly regularly and knew there was Oscar buzz around his last film, a documentary in which he traveled to Colombia and collected jungle sounds from brooks, waterfalls, insects, the rain, the birds, the wind in the trees, the reflection of trees on the water, tides rushing and emptying, piles of shells on beaches, water being collected in plastic tubs. Its debut at Cannes was met with a seven-minute standing ovation.

Nathaniel and I had interacted a few more times since I first asked him to tie my shoe, but I didn't tell Delphine that yet. Whenever Nathaniel came by the Peabody to see his thesis advisor, Dr. Deborah Murphy, we would hurl lines at each other at the front desk for a few precious moments, always intended to provoke, to generate more attention the next time. It didn't take long for Nathaniel to tell me that he spent every summer in Colombia as a child. He knew the food. He knew the slang. He knew the culture well.

"Did you know he's a legacy, too?" Delphine teased. "His parents *met* here."

"I told him he only talked to me because I was pretty and charismatic and he said I wasn't that charismatic."

Delphine laughed. "That's very mean."

It was way past midnight, and Delphine decided to crash with me. It felt cozy to know that we were young and could always go somewhere to drink more or watch *Pulp Fiction* and talk daringly about cocaine but succumb to the reality of french fries from the late-night kitchen downstairs run by sophomores.

We put in an order for cheese fries and went up to my room to wait. I took off my bra facing away from Delphine and put on a

Led Zeppelin shirt from Urban Outfitters with Six Flags parking lot speed.

She looked at the postcards of writers I had taped to my wall. She frowned.

"God, not Woody Allen," she said.

I felt wholesome with Delphine, like a child. Maybe I would tell her I had never flown a kite, had never wanted to, but had she? Was it fun? And she'd say, *Yeah, kind of.* What happens if it flies away? Like how when birthday balloons fly away. And we would sit in silence. Then I would ask her more questions. *What are the different kinds of melon?* I would ask her if she was impressed I could drink almost as much as her dad and she would say, Yes, yes she was, she bet I'd probably always be able to.

I dragged my laptop from my desk to the bed and pulled up Facebook. Delphine climbed next to me as we searched for Nathaniel's profile. We saw pictures of him with a girl I assumed was his ex. You don't need a description of her. It's a police sketch of a pretty white girl. A yard sale watercolor of the first day of spring. I wondered why, when this creature could do anything in the world, be anything, have anything, why she had wanted what she wanted—*him.*

"It says he's single," teased Delphine. "Do you like him?"

I ignored the question and instead choked up the furball that had been stuck in my throat all night long.

"Next week the DREAM Act is going to be debated in the Senate." I had intended to sound more breezy than I did. I rolled onto my back and stared up at the ceiling.

"Fuck," she said softly.

I was in the seventh grade when I first heard of the DREAM Act. The bill was in the news, and my grandfather decided it was time for me to know the truth. He just told me one day. He grabbed me by the shoulders and said, "You overstayed your visa. You don't have papers. But don't worry. There's a law that's going to pass soon that will allow you to study here and become a citizen." He handed me a copy of *The New York Times* picked up at the corner Egyptian bodega folded perfectly to reveal an article on the DREAM Act. He ruffled my hair supportively. I just stared at him. I was already an orphan and an at-risk youth; this all felt like a lot.

The Development, Relief, and Education for Alien Minors (DREAM) Act had been around since 2001. It was initially a bipartisan bill promising a path to legal status for undocumented young people who came to this country as children. *Dreamers.* The bill was introduced, revised, filibustered, repackaged, disappeared, and then introduced again for years, it was honestly hard to keep track. In September of my freshman year at Harvard, when the U.S. military was hungry for new recruits, a version of the DREAM Act was included as an amendment to a defense spending bill. Military leaders were hopeful. But Dick Durbin, one of the architects of the original act, was heavily criticized for peddling around this shadier version, so the amendment was tabled. Then one month later, he introduced it in the Senate again, where it fell just eight votes short of breaking the filibuster.

At the time, I'd been so overcome by fear and paralysis that I'd done nothing at all but watch from a distance alone. Having seen the typhoon of xenophobia and nationalism after 9/11, I knew better than to be optimistic, even if the military saw Dreamers as an untapped resource. Now, Dick Durbin was back and at it again. The DREAM Act, along with a repeal of "Don't Ask, Don't Tell," had been tacked onto a big defense bill. On September 21, the Senate would be taking a vote. All we needed was sixty votes.

"The Dreamers are throwing a vigil outside of City Hall tomorrow," I said. "I want to go but I don't think I can go alone. What would I do alone?"

I could almost hear Delphine's heart drop. Our friendship had been strained by my hurt over her refusal to vote, and this wasn't voting, but it *was* political.

But a genuine warm and lovely smile spread on her face. "I'll go with you."

I didn't want to be out about my status for many reasons—fear, pride, the fact that my dream was to be an exceedingly serious and important capital-A artist the likes of which the world had never seen before and there was no chance of that happening if I became an undocumented poster girl. I could see, from the outside, how someone might think I would be good for the job, but that's because they didn't know shit about me. Still, if the DREAM Act somehow did pass, I didn't want to look back and realize I had done nothing to fight for the bill. I had, in fact, done nothing— none of the teach-ins, sit-ins, hunger strikes, phone banking, or risky media appearances—but if it passed, I would benefit from all of that labor anyhow. I'd be able to have a life.

We woke up late, got dressed, picked up Olsen Twin–size soy vanilla lattes at Starbucks, and took a quiet T ride to City Hall together. Neither of us attempted small talk.

On the steps outside of City Hall there was a small gathering of mostly Latine young people. They were writing their names and dreams with Sharpies on a huge American flag they planned to send to Senator Scott Brown, who was rumored to be voting no even though he had been the replacement senator when Ted Kennedy died and the DREAM Act had been one of Ted Kennedy's personal pet projects.

Someone handed us candles in white foam cups. As soon as Delphine got hers, we turned to each other and sang a whispery and giggly rendition of "Will You Light My Candle?" from the official cast recording of *Rent* performed by Daphne Rubin-Vega and Adam Pascal. Somewhere after Mimi drips wax on Roger but before Roger recognizes Mimi from the Cat Scratch Club, Delphine's long hair caught fire on my candle and she screamed and I screamed louder and we both swatted at her head quite violently until the fire was gone and only the putrid smell of burnt hair remained. One of the Dreamers, a tall kid in skinny jeans and red Converse, walked over to me and said, "I'll take this," revoking candle privileges.

I couldn't bear to look at the other Dreamers for too long. I felt so much love for them, and it made me sad to see them try to keep hope. What scared me was overhearing the word *when,* as in *When the DREAM Act passes I'll finally be able to . . .* When. They were stupid for believing. I'd stopped believing so, so long ago, it didn't even make me feel moody and contrarian. It just was what it was.

Later that week I watched C-SPAN's live coverage of the DREAM Act vote with my laptop on mute while I was sitting in seminar. A banner popped up announcing what I already knew—the DREAM Act was filibustered, it was not going in for a vote, and my professor—almost on cue, his timing was so fucking precise—said, "If most Latin American countries were wiped off the face of the Earth, it would not cause a dent in the lives of Americans." We were just four votes short.

The DRCLAS awards ceremony and reception was that night. Nathaniel, golden boy of Anthro, was there, too. He seemed to know everyone. When he spotted me, he waved and held up a finger as an old lady with lavender-toned white hair grabbed his face and kissed him on both cheeks. He was making rounds, and he'd be with me in just a moment.

"Hello, Catalina," he said, joining me at the top of the stairs.

"Nathaniel."

"It's nice to see you here. I'm glad you came."

"Thank you, I am also happy to see you here and I am also glad you came."

"You look nice."

"Thank you. If you had left without talking to me, the evening would have been a complete waste of a dress."

"What do you mean?"

"Because you saw—" I caught myself smiling sincerely. "You've put me in the position of having to explain my joke."

"Go ahead, I'm listening."

"Well, if you had left without talking to me, the evening would have been a waste of a dress because you hadn't seen me in it."

He laughed. "Not your best work."

"Why are you here?"

"Why are any of us here?"

Together, we leaned forward against the staircase railing of the second floor, looking at the people, exchanging dozens of lies but no insincerities, our voices sharp and bright like shattered disco ball powder. I thought about how good it would feel to throw myself over the railing, kids go splat under the chandelier. I wouldn't die. It would feel like a good stretch, maybe, to have some bones broken.

A tall older woman walked by Nathaniel and gripped his shoulder.

"Atta boy," she said in a low voice by way of greeting.

Nathaniel in turn put a hand on her shoulder and said, "Professor Murphy, this is Catalina."

"Catalina! My pleasure. Deborah Murphy." She offered me her hand.

She needed no introduction. Dr. Murphy was a world-renowned expert in the khipu, a stringed recording device used by the Inca. She had a reputation for dressing eccentrically. Tonight, she was rocking three clashing patterns, a blue, yellow, and red tartan suit jacket over an argyle cashmere vest over a blue and bluer striped button-down shirt partially unbuttoned. She was basically a celebrity at the Peabody.

The museum actually owned a handful of khipus, a handful out of the hundreds that are housed in museums and private collections around the world. The khipu relied on knots and strings to record accounting data necessary for the management of a large and growing empire: agricultural figures, storehouse inventories, census information, taxes. It's possible they were also used to record poetry, celestial maps, genealogies, military reports, legal code. Potentially everything. In the Andes, very few people knew how to make and read khipus. They were called quipucamayocs, a priestly class in many ways, and because they held the power of documentation, they often had run-ins with the king. Before the Spanish invaded, King Atahualpa had, let's say, an *expansionist* diplomatic policy. It wasn't just the Inca people in that region, there were many other tribes, and they were often at war. Whenever he conquered a new group of people and forced them to become Inca, Atahualpa ordered that the people's quipucamayocs be killed and ordered that their khipus be burned. He wanted to control the narrative. He wanted history to belong to him. He wanted to erase their memories. He really wanted them gone. *There,* working, paying taxes, but *gone.* This was not the last time quipucamayocs were met with violence by a power-hungry regime. When the Spanish invaded, they burned as many khipus as they wanted to and killed the quipucamayocs, too.

Archaeologists and anthropologists have found and collected a number of stringed survivors, but they don't definitively know how to decipher the khipu's system of knots, strings, and fibers. Since at least the sixteenth century, the mystery of the khipu has continued to drive people mad. Do the color and origin of the fibers or thickness of the bright ribbons hide meaning? Could the knots represent more than numbers—perhaps syllables, sounds, symbols, words, or could they be melodies? Do all khipus even adhere to the same principles? Entire worlds of ideas, beliefs, histories, all hidden in ever enigmatic spreadsheets. Nobody has been able to crack the code. The closest anyone had ever gotten was Dr. Murphy.

In part thanks to her leadership, Harvard was something of a hotbed for khipu decoders. Mathematicians, historians, theologists, anthropologists, archaeologists, linguists. Some built digital databases and computer programs for decoding. Others excavated burial grounds. Everyone was after the same thing: They wanted to find a "rosetta khipu," the khipu to unlock all others. The upcoming spring exhibition at the Peabody, *The Khipu and Its Infinite Possibilities,* an ode to the mystery, would include khipus on loan from as far as Berlin and Peru. A big event banner was already hanging by the front desk.

"I was just telling Catalina about your research," Nathaniel lied. "Catalina is from Ecuador."

No, not this.

"Really! What part of Ecuador are you from?"

"Cotopaxi."

"I've never been, but I bet it's beautiful. Of course I've been to Ecuador many times, but my work takes me deep in the highlands. It's a stunningly beautiful country."

"So I've heard," I said.

"Were you not born there?"

"No, I *was* born there. I just haven't been back in a long time."

"Oh! Why not?"

"Family drama," I said vaguely. "Don't even get me started."

I felt Dr. Murphy's curious eyes on me and instinctively put my shoulders back and lifted my chin. She could look through my bunker all she wanted, she wasn't finding a thing. The effect of my withholding on other people was fascinating. Typically, the more distant I was with them, the more passionately they pursued a relationship I'm not even sure they wanted.

Before the Spanish turned on the khipu, they actually encouraged its usage, imagining that the mysterious system of strings and knots could be adapted for the accounting of things like baptisms, confessions, and conversions. The Mercedarian missionaries even ordered that all the newly conquered indigenous people have their own personal *prayer khipus*. If they didn't, they'd get lashings. Meanwhile, the Jesuit missionaries were obsessed with confession and ordered the indigenous people of the Andes to keep *confessional khipus* for recording sins such as noticing a woman and desiring to sin with her, as well as harboring, in one's heart, the desire to harm a priest. Local quipucamayocs were appointed to function as informants, go-betweens between indigenous people and the Church. They would meet with members of their community, collect their sins, and then make confessional khipus to narrate back to the Spaniards. But the quipucamayocs resisted when they could, they counseled their friends and neighbors through the whole thing, giving them tips on what to say and how to say it. Sometimes the same khipu was used for multiple people's confessions. In addition to that, Church officials became suspicious when they learned that khipus recorded offerings to non-Christian gods. This angered the Spanish. To make matters worse, they had caught wind that private khipu transmissions could be used to coordinate rebellions, right under their noses. Eventually, the Church declared the khipu idolatrous, and that's when they killed the quipucamayocs and ordered all khipus burned.

"Dr. Murphy, if I may ask, what got you interested in the Andes?"

Dr. Murphy chuckled and took a small sip of her wine, looking happy and deep in thought. I had a feeling this would be the right question to ask.

"I'm an old lady, Catalina. You think I can remember that far back?"

I tilted my head to the side and smiled.

"I'll tell you the truth, there was this one moment when I was in graduate school, many lifetimes ago. The village I was in was high, high, high up in the mountains in Peru, and on the way down I encountered a family throwing a big party for their daughter's birthday, and the syncretism of it all, the Catholicism, the ancient rituals, the African drums, the Native American flutes, the Spanish ballads, the pink princess dress. The family was just so welcoming. The father placed his daughter on my lap. It all made sense somehow, and I fell in love with fieldwork there and then. There's nothing like it."

I could feel the muscles in my face twitch from holding a smile. I excused myself, claimed my award money, and walked home alone.

In romantic comedies, when two lovers meet, one of them asks the other to promise they won't fall in love. Invariably, they fall in love. One morning, when Nathaniel stopped by the front desk of the Peabody, I decided to try it. I was curious about what he'd say. Anything he said would be a surprise, either his answer would make me happy or it would make me sad, but whatever it was, it was *something*. Nothing was happening and I was curious about what I could make happen out of thin air.

To be specific, I had decided I wanted to experience heartbreak. Heartbreak was probably even more famous than love. Songs about heartbreak, for example, were famously better than

ones about domestic bliss, and Camilo had been a disappoint-
ment. All the poets were heartbroken and in a state of perpetual
losing and longing. The way Dante thought about Beatrice—
lustful, obsessive, theatrical—is how I thought about absolutely
everything.

"Don't fall in love with me," I said.

"What?"

"Promise you won't fall in love with me."

"Catalina," he started, then paused for a long time, and
smirked, leaving my name unattended in the air.

"Something tells me that if I seriously pursued you, I'd be a
trope in your life. And fuck if I'm going to be a trope in someone
else's story."

I was hurt and laughed wildly. I grasped for an insult.

"What are you doing after graduation, *consulting*?" In my
mouth the word was poison.

But then he said, "Come out with me this weekend."

"So you can be a trope in my life story?"

"Among other things," he said. "It's my classmate's birthday
Saturday. Kirkland House, *Secret Garden* themed. Come with
me."

Nathaniel slurred slightly when he spoke, like his mouth was
full of honey, a kitten mid-yawn. If I made my eyes glaze over, like
really glaze over, he looked like the drummer from the Strokes.

"Fine. You can pick me up at ten." I wanted it to be a date, and
I wanted him to have to wait for me.

Nathaniel lived in Eliot House, which is by the Charles River,
so in order to pick me up he would either need to take a shuttle
or walk a good twenty minutes to my dorm on the Quad. Then
from there, we would have to retrace his steps because Kirkland
House, the location of the party, was also a dorm by the Charles

River; in fact, it was right next to Eliot House. None of this occurred to me when I made my ask, nor when he agreed.

On Saturday, the dining hall opened at 4:30 P.M. and I went
down at five. Every party invite made me feel like Cinderella,
touched by magic, going to the ball as a fugitive, a wanted woman.
I had meatloaf and mashed potatoes. I ate *so* well when I was in
college. I still sometimes think about how well I ate. I had an ice
cream float at almost every dinner. I microwaved brownies and
ate them warm with vanilla ice cream. I tried macaroni & cheese
and meatloaf for the first time. I can't say that I liked the flavor,
but I don't really think American cuisine is about flavor, it's like a
stand against communism. Meatloaf wasn't good but it didn't
need to be good—it put me inside a cozy Norman Rockwell
painting and that was enough. Other times, it was not enough,
and I felt a gnawing, painful hunger but couldn't think of a single
food I actually wanted. I was so hungry but had already decided
no food would satisfy me, nothing sweet, nothing savory. For a
minute I wondered if what I wanted was sex, but then realized
that what I wanted was to punish everyone who ever laid a finger
on me.

Henry Kissinger is a man of no small imagination, and unbe-
knownst to me, he and the other Henries were hard at work on a
dress. He can get excited, Mr. Kissinger. As you know, his weakness has always been Swarovski crystals. He wanted to hand-sew
twenty-two thousand Swarovski crystals onto a whisper of a dress
on loan from Chanel; as I have explained, his hands are small and
also nimble.

"Twenty-two thousand crystals!" I exclaimed incredulously.
"At your age? Why would you do such a thing?"

"It's because I love you and admire you, Ms. Catalina," said
Henry. "You are beautiful and I am a fool."

"Oh, Henry!"

I added a plastic rose stolen from the dining hall to my hair to stay on theme.

My beauty trick at the time was scrunching my hair with loads of rosehip Herbal Essences conditioner right before I went out and tying it on top of my head in a knot. When I took my hair down later that night, I would smell like a dream and a flower. Another thing I'd do was stop the dryer cycle midway so that my clothes were damp and more formfitting. Plus, I'd also smell like fresh laundry, a scent proven to elicit a promising psychosexual response in most constitutions.

The Latinas I grew up around were mostly Puerto Rican and Dominican and I idolized them. They smelled good. Every inch of their skin was moisturized. Their hair looked wet from morning showers, from gel, from mousse and hairspray. Their nails were done, their toes were done, their edges were neat. The older women wore matching platinum and diamond engagement rings and wedding bands. I imagined them pointing a square acrylic nail at their boss and saying, "No." They probably didn't, but I imagined they did. Sonia Sotomayor was sworn in as a Supreme Court justice, as the first Latina Supreme Court justice, in 2009, my sophomore year. Sotomayor was briefed about her appearance and encouraged to wear a neutral nail to her swearing in. No bright colors. She took that advice but then wore red nail polish to the White House reception held in her honor, and showed them off to the president. *No.*

Nathaniel was outside my dorm at exactly ten. I was seven minutes late. Harvard had a tradition of starting everything seven minutes after the hour, even classes. I did not understand why Harvard had the seven-minute-late tradition and seemed to be inept at understanding when I should and should not observe it.

"You look really nice," he said when he saw me. I wore a

dreamy chiffon minidress with delicate spaghetti straps the same color as my eyeshadow, kitten paw pink. Now, when I say chiffon, I do mean polyester, and thanks for asking, yes, yes, crystals *everywhere*!

Now that I had Nathaniel's attention, I had no idea what to do with it. He was looking at me and I was looking at myself being looked at. It's a powerful thing, being an object, but it's boring. All you have to do is sit there. If I was born to be an object, #98 on the call sheet, understudy to the white girls, Tijuana for the boys, I could at least take creative control. I could make myself into something to behold, like the golden calf and the wrath of Moses. I, too, could quote Charles Bukowski. I could wear headbands. Learn to drink port. You can be whoever you want in America.

"My rabbi friended me on Facebook last night," he said as we started to walk to Kirkland House. "I spent all morning scrubbing my profile of anything remotely offensive."

"I can make it offensive again," I said, too quickly.

We both seemed unsure of what to say next.

"Do you know the story about Evita's body?" he blurted out. "It's like my favorite story ever."

"No, I don't. Tell me," I said.

"I swear, a single corpse has never been through so much. Perón wanted to have her embalmed and then he wanted to display her in a monument—like Lenin—so he ordered that her body be embalmed but before the monument is completed there's the coup and Perón flees, abandoning Evita's corpse. The body disappears. No one knows where it is for fifteen years. Then in the seventies, they find her body in a crypt in Italy under an entirely different name and send it to Perón in Spain—by the way Perón is now remarried and he and his new wife put Evita's body in their *dining room.* Swear to god."

"Damn," I said.

"I know, right?"

"Where is her body now?"

"Buenos Aires. I've seen it. Or rather, I've seen the decoy coffin that is on top of a trapdoor. Her real coffin is in a vault deep underground. No way to steal it now."

Nathaniel wanted to take over my grandfather's spot at the head of the table, condemned forever to the first slice of cake, the choice cut from the roasted bird, the final say. I just wanted him to kiss me.

Now, I do not fault Nathaniel for having been hopelessly drawn to my continent and its neighboring islands, isthmuses, and peninsulas. I understand the allure myself. But for all his love of exotic, sensuous, beautiful Latin America, Nathaniel didn't seem too interested in Latine people. He didn't have very many friends like me, did he? Real friends, not ethnographic subjects. He knew all about Bartolomé de Las Casas, and he could quote Sor Juana from memory, but in the world order narrated to me by my grandfather, we were migrants, we were exiles, we were anointed, we were people protected by God, and people like Nathaniel and his friends were tourists.

"So, you live with your grandparents?" he asked after another pause in conversation. "What do they do?"

"My grandma is a nanny and my grandfather owns a construction company."

"Oh, awesome," he said. "That is *really* cool."

The truth, that my grandmother didn't work but occasionally babysat for neighbors, and that my grandfather was aging out of being a construction worker, was not something Nathaniel had earned.

I let another moment of silence settle.

"I've never told you about my thesis research, have I?"

My heart sank. I already knew Nathaniel's focus in anthropology was the Andes. That was enough.

"No," I said. "I've been meaning to ask you."

"So, for me, it's frustrating to hear people say the Inca Empire is somehow inferior to other empires of similar reach because they did not have a writing system." He scoffed. "But the Inca Empire was actually incredibly sophisticated, at the time, in the sixteenth century, it was one of the biggest empires in the world so they obviously had sophisticated methods of running their society. One of those methods was—okay, imagine a mop. It's called a khipu."

He held out his arm.

"Let's say this is the parent cord. Okay?"

I wanted him to stop talking, and he'd do that sooner if I pretended to know nothing.

"Now, picture a bunch of strings hanging from this arm, and each one of those strings has knots. Those strings can also have their own strings with their own knots, those are called subsidiary cords. Let me know if this is too boring."

"No, not at all. It's super interesting."

"The strings can be made of llama wool, alpaca wool, they can be dyed, there are knots made to the left, knots turned to the right, there's almost an infinite number of ways the knots can be differentiated from each other. It's definitely an accounting system, but I think it's a written language, too. Advanced civilizations are supposed to have written languages, right? This is it. So my project is an ethnographic study of this village in the highlands in Peru where some very old khipus have been found. That's where all the oldest ones come from because the arid climate has preserved them perfectly. Here's where I come in. I'll be going around to the eldest members of the community and making a record of what they know, what embodied knowledge may have been passed down. We don't want to lose that. If one person who knows information about how a khipu can be read dies, that knowledge dies with them. Imagine."

"What do the knots feel like?" I asked.

"They're so old, you can't really touch them without damaging them."

"But that's the point, touching it, isn't it? You told me the strings were different fibers, llama, alpaca. How can you tell what they are unless you touch them?"

"If you're trained, you don't have to touch them to know."

"I don't think you're right," I said softly.

"I don't know what to do about you," he said.

At the party, we made the rounds to say hello to everyone Nathaniel knew. I quickly realized it was more of a jeans and fleece pullover situation than what I'd imagined and I suddenly felt self-conscious about the amount of body glitter I was wearing. Nathaniel greeted all the girls with an air kiss on the cheek and the guys with a dap. His girl friends held out their arms and hugged me warmly. "So you're the famous Catalina!" I felt flattered and humiliated. I wanted to be loved and admired, but I did not want to be talked about.

In the middle of the room someone had set up a white canopy over a wheeled-in couch draped with plastic flowers. People went in there to mess around. A dance remix of Neil Young's "Harvest Moon" abruptly segued into Kanye West. It was my first time seeing white people dance outside of television and for what it's worth I thought it was very brave.

When I got to Harvard I expected dance parties to look like a scene from *Save the Last Dance* or *Honey*, my go-to references for youthful gatherings. The only other example I had was congregation parties. Congregation parties were usually potlucks held at a dance hall and the occasions were anniversaries, graduations, baby showers, weddings. While actual holidays were prohibited, parties were not. Again, every sister in the congregation had a specialty and they made it for every party. My grandmother's specialty was Ecuadorian ceviche, Sister Rosa's was Peruvian ceviche, and Sister Anita's was macaroni salad with ham. Sister Suarez made potato salad with green apple. Sister Matos made arroz con gandules. Sister Morales's specialty was pernil. Sister Miranda's was pupusas. The dancing was as pan-Latin as the food was. We danced bachata, merengue, cumbias from both Colombia and Mexico, quebradita, the Ecuadorian sanjuanito, whatever cursed genre the electric slide falls under. The one thing that they did not play was reggaeton. Too sexy.

Nathaniel wanted to dance but I was nowhere near drunk enough to do that. I wasn't drunk at all. I felt grouchy.

"Why don't you want to dance?"

"I do want to dance, I just don't want to dance to this song. It's making me feel nothing."

"Okay, next one?"

"Depends on what it is and how it makes me feel."

I stood around like a wallflower, unmoved by the treble, unwet by the bass, annoying the hell out of Nathaniel when I decided to leave.

"I forgot I have to do something for my grandma—I have to do it by midnight. I'm so sorry but I really got to go."

Nathaniel looked surprised.

"Yeah, yeah yeah, of course. Do you need anything? You okay walking back alone?"

I was already out the door.

I threw myself in bed without washing my face. Oh, relief! I was finally back in my single, a quiet, dark room with a door that locked automatically. I took off my clothes and climbed into bed. I was wide-awake, my mind racing. WikiLeaks was all over the news. The leak pertaining to the Iraq War revealed that between 60 and 80 percent of the war casualties were civilian deaths. I thought about how heavily the army recruited at my high school. What Goldman Sachs was to Harvard seniors is what the U.S. Army was to me and my high school classmates. Look at them, three hulking, perfectly postured service members with sign-up sheets and graphs illustrating how much the army contributes to their veterans' education. So Dr. Kissinger or one of the other guys says, "Let's bomb this place," but they don't actually do it; the sick motherfuckers get poor kids to do it. It made sense. My grandfather had told me this is how the world worked.

At around three in the morning I got a text from Nathaniel.

Let me take you on a proper date.

I hadn't even given him my number. I felt desired, the most amazing feeling in the world.

You just want to fuck me.

He responded quickly.

No, not at all.

Then after several minutes:

Do you want me to fuck you?

I tossed my phone face down on the floor and finally went to sleep.

The first week of November, I auditioned to join the campus literary magazine, *The Harvard Advocate,* colloquially known as *The Advo*. I did not necessarily want to be on the editorial board, nor did I intend to contribute to the magazine, but I did want to put myself through the competition so I could see myself be scored. I was addicted to being evaluated. Something about being passed through so many hands as a child, something about not knowing why exactly I had been shipped off to America, made me feel like any value I was ever going to have I had to accrue myself, coin by coin, like *Donkey Kong*. Intellectually I knew that I had innate God-given worth, everyone did, all of us, even the non-sentient flora that terrified me, but the loss made a permanent mark. My brain had been new and young and soft, and so it froze in time that way, it froze in time and extralinguistic terror like the dogs from Pompeii. I ran away from the feeling as much as I could, and one way of doing that was putting myself up to be graded, evaluated, judged, selected, awarded, and—of course—*chosen* as much as possible. It worked, when it worked, like a charm.

The comp was on a Wednesday. I remember because it was the day after the midterm elections. I watched in horror as the Republicans swept the House. It was embarrassingly transparent that behind this stunning sweep were white Americans triggered by how smart, beautiful, rich, fit, charismatic, cool, and popular Barack and Michelle Obama were. They erupted in envy.

At the introductory meeting, which was like a combination of a group interview and an exam, the editors sat cross-legged on tables. Vida, a small South Asian girl with flared jeans and red ballet flats, introduced herself as editor of the Fiction board and she began the meeting by reading through the names of past alumni. This happened at a lot of first meetings at Harvard and the names could get ridiculous.

"As many of you know, *The Harvard Advocate* is the oldest arts and letters student magazine in the United States. Former editors have included John Ashbery, Frank O'Hara, Seamus Heaney, T. S. Eliot, and e. e. cummings. A real rainbow coalition of old white men." We laughed. "Let's try to wrap this up," she said, and ran through the names in an impatient, weary monotone, like we were absolutely burdened to be the certain heirs to these great and brilliant men, like it was annoying.

Of course I thought Henry Kissinger was brilliant. Boring men don't interest me. He was an immigrant child with a traumatic past making his way up the ladder in America. Let's say I felt a kinship. And he had a heck of a story. Kissinger was fifteen years old when he fled Nazi Germany. He applied for asylum in the United States, got asylum, was naturalized as a citizen, and not long after that he joined the army and returned to Germany as an American soldier. As far as American Dream stories go, that one's pretty good. It made me feel almost competitive.

Vida then passed out two stories, both short, and asked us to read them and be ready to discuss. The first story was a very serious story about two young men in love, and there was a lot of sex in it, and a lot of fighting. It was clear that this was a serious story. The second story was about a garden snake that eats a puppy.

After ensuring we had all completed the readings, Vida cleared her throat and spoke up: "So, which story would you publish and why?"

I pulled the neck of my shirt up to cover the bottom half of my face. I felt compelled to like the serious story, and that felt suffocating. One of those stories was literature, one was not. Who were they to decide? We! I was one of them.

The boys spoke first. The room felt tense, not because there was any disagreement over which story was more publishable but because they were all trying to top one another. I couldn't stand it. It wasn't what they said. It was in the delivery, how definitive and final their words felt, how dogmatic. How joyless. This shit wasn't even real. It didn't even matter. I scanned the room and tried to identify who I thought would become a corporate lawyer and then imagined them wearing ugly gray *suits*.

"Catalina," Vida said, reading my name tag, "do you have any thoughts? It's okay if you don't."

I froze. Then I took a breath in, sat up straighter, and said a quick, panicked prayer in my head. If I declined the opportunity to comment, I'd be acquiescing to the suggestion that I might not have thoughts. But I *didn't* have thoughts. I had *feelings*. I had angry feelings. What was I supposed to say? *I hate your stupid opinions on art because you grew up with cable? I will never take you seriously because your family owns a vacation home?* On the exhale, I heard myself begin to speak.

"I think the story that deserves to be published in the anthology is the puppy/snake story. The way I see it, some of us have been sexualized since we were really young and didn't get a chance to be children, so we may want the anthology to be a children's book for college students. How about a coloring book? *Puppy and Snake.* It can come with an accompanying CD, like how some issues of *The Believer* have CDs? Like that. As for music, I'm thinking Raffi. Just a bunch of Raffi in there. Interviews with Raffi, a photo essay on a day in the life of a little brown whale on the go."

I stopped abruptly. "So that's my vote." I closed my eyes and tried to untighten my stomach.

Nobody laughed. I thought *some* parts were funny. The silence was a mixture of confusion, annoyance, discomfort, and a reluctance to contradict me because I was the only Latina in the room. Then somebody laughed. I looked around.

"I'm thoroughly convinced," Kyle said from the back of the room, raising his hand with a proud smile.

I did not make it past the first round.

✳ •

Before Nathaniel and I had that "proper date" he'd asked for, he invited me to have lunch with him and his father who was coming into town for the Harvard-Yale football game. Harvard had beat Yale for the past nine consecutive years and all sorts of alumni were coming in to potentially see win numero diez. Meeting his father before sleeping with him felt wrong, but this is how boys are sometimes. They get excited. Mr. Wheeler made a reservation at the Endnote, a fancy restaurant where people got engaged and where wealthy parents made reservations for graduation years in advance. I couldn't help but feel those famous apocryphal butterflies flutter around in my belly. Did I want to be Nathaniel's girlfriend? No. I wanted him to fuck me. Him particularly. Something about the hard turn upward of his chin. I could take or leave the rest but that I loved. It could make me shy.

My chief preoccupation was with what to wear. Childhood religious trauma had made me all but allergic to modest clothing. But maybe I could try this time. Maybe I could try to be a good girl. I wondered if it would feel nice to be loved by a boy. What did that feel like?

I arrived at the Endnote wearing a sleeveless short black dress with a white pilgrim collar. I blew out my hair and wore a thin black velvet headband, feeling the part of a lovely young woman with a bright future and impeccable table manners, maybe a second cousin of Wednesday Addams. Nathaniel kissed me formally on the cheek, grabbed my hand, and said, "He's upstairs."

I was terrified to meet Byron Wheeler. He was an iconoclast. An auteur. I wondered if, when he saw me, he'd imagine me having sex with his son. What did fathers think about?

The place was nice—everything looked rich and old, lots of dark oak and polished, constantly polished, polished, polished by someone, polished by whom.

Nathaniel led me to a corner table, and he said, beaming, "This is Catalina."

"Catalina, it is *really* great to meet you. Call me Byron." He stood up. He stuck out his hand and I leaned in instinctively for a hug instead.

Mr. Wheeler had a totally shaved head and he wore thick-framed glasses, parachute pants, and Gucci loafers. I'd never met such a delightfully dressed heterosexual.

I am generally good with parents, perfect manners, polite conversation. I know how to land a well-placed giggle. Byron wanted to hear about my essay prize, it was an academic accomplishment, parents like that. Then the server came up to ask if we wanted to start with cocktails or perhaps a bottle of wine.

The server was a Latino man. He was dressed like a penguin. He wordlessly poured sparkling water from what looked like a glass vase.

I smiled a wide, toothy, dumb valedictorian smile and said, "I can pour my own water, thank you." I took the vase from the man's hands and sloppily, nervously, poured myself some lukewarm water. There was total silence. When I handed the carafe back to the stunned and embarrassed man, I glanced at his name tag.

"Julio. I'm Catalina. Nice to meet you."

Nathaniel looked at his father. Byron Wheeler looked at me. As soon as Julio walked away, he leaned toward me and said, "I'm sure the staff earns above the minimum wage here, they've been beloved members of the community for a long time—"

"Dad," Nathaniel interrupted, "it's not a big deal. Catalina is just funny like that."

"I don't want her to get the wrong impression," he said with a shrug.

"I don't think she thinks anything bad, do you, Catalina?" Nathaniel asked.

"I like to serve myself, that's all," I said quietly. "Mrs. Dalloway said she would buy the flowers herself. You know?"

I rolled my eyes, trying again. "It's a feminist thing!" I said with exaggerated vocal fry.

Byron Wheeler looked at me with his mouth slightly ajar and his eyebrows slightly raised, but eventually he laughed a little and then he laughed a lot. This was the first time, but it would not be the last, that I would not stand to be served by men who looked like my grandfather.

"You grew up Catholic, right?"

I said yes.

"I can see a Catholic girl a mile away," he said. "It's the guilt."

"That's what they say," I said. "That's what they say."

"Now, Catalina, you're going to have to tell me if you can figure this one out. Okay? It's a funny story. Are you ready?"

I smiled. "Yes."

"Anytime I meet an older Ecuadorian woman, anywhere in the world, she ends up asking me to marry her daughter, like, right away. Of course I say I'm a happily married man. And they insist, they take my hand, and they say, 'Just meet her, just see her.' And then it happens again and again. It happens everywhere. It happened inside the supermarket in Quito, it happened a few months

ago at a completely random laundromat in Bogotá, I was picking
up my laundry and this short lady, clearly a matriarch, barely four
feet, ten inches, name was María—this is the second María to do
this, by the way—she says, 'Let me introduce you to my daughter.' I cannot be going crazy. My batting average is, like, off the
charts. So you have to tell me. Is this insane? Is there something
to this? I'm the son of a statistician, and my inclination is to think
it is not a coincidence. It's madness."

"That's funny," I said. "It's really funny. It's like you didn't exist
before, and now you suddenly do."

Nathaniel was laughing, he was in agreement, this was a funny
story. He looked small next to his father, like a dollhouse minia-
ture of a man.

✳ •

My uncle Patricio, my second father, died in Ecuador the last
week of November. He died of a heart attack at forty-five. It was
just after Thanksgiving. I was home on break when we received
the call. When she heard the news, my grandmother's wail was
terrifyingly animal. My grandfather's face turned white, and he
went silent. My grandmother shook him to get him to speak but
he refused.

I knew this was coming, it happens to every undocumented
person in America. It is simply a matter of time. A close family
member back home dies. You are unable to leave this country,
unable to travel home, to say goodbye, to bury your dead. You can
afford a calling card but, try as you might to influence the funeral
arrangements, you're not there. You're in one of those nightmares
where you scream and scream and nobody can hear you. It was
our turn now.

I understood that my job was to not betray how I was feeling
in any way. I missed my aunt for a long time after I started living

in America, but if I ever mentioned her my grandmother burst
into tears because I still hadn't called *her* "mami." So I stopped
bringing my aunt and uncle up altogether. I tried to feel nothing
about Ecuador. It wasn't easy. I welled up when I heard Andean
flutists outside the T in Harvard Square perform a Celine Dion/
Carlos Vives medley. That was mine, somehow. It was almost
mine.

My uncle's death confirmed all of my grandfather's fears about
himself and his place in the family. He could not protect. He
could not provide. Emasculation at the hands of the state is a very
cunning thing for the state to do because men will never see it
coming from the state. They'll blame the subjects in their own
kingdoms, the women and children to whom they are lords. The
only people to whom they are lords.

My grandfather grew darker as the days got shorter. I returned
to Boston to finish my last week of classes before reading week
and finals, and he landed himself in two physical fights with total
strangers all before the weekend even came around. To be fair,
both guys deserved to be smacked. One guy called him "a fucking
Mexican" outside a Home Depot, and the other guy, according to
him at least, was an old man hitting on a teenage girl at the bus
stop. I would have wanted to punch them, too. Of course, we
can't always do what we want to do, especially when we are undocumented, because when police get involved, ICE gets involved and there goes your life. I thought about this every day of
my entire life. I didn't even jaywalk. But here was my grandfather
being the hero.

He was drinking brown liquor deep into the night and listening to melancholy songs, boleros and vals and Ecuadorian pasil-
los, particularly a subgenre whose entire point is to make you feel
like dying, colloquially it's called musica corta venas, which I'm
too squeamish to translate. The music made him nostalgic and

the more nostalgic my grandfather got, the more he drank. My grandmother called me on Saturday morning to complain about how late he came in the night before, how strongly he smelled like rum, how he didn't even brush his teeth before going to bed.

"I don't know what you want me to do," I said. "I live in Massachusetts. It's a whole other state!"

"Just come home, Catalina."

"I'll be home in a few weeks," I half-heartedly protested. "The semester is almost over!"

"Catalina, please. Talk to him. Now. He'll listen to you." My grandmother was convinced that I was all-powerful when it came to my grandfather. Whatever it was, she was convinced I could solve it. It also occurred to me that maybe she didn't want to be alone with him.

I agreed to go home the first weekend of December, and then I agreed to do it again the next. I felt embarrassed about going home so much, just like I had done my freshman year when I was overwhelmed by the sudden separation, but it felt crazy to be stuck in Cambridge while my grandfather spiraled. I didn't tell Delphine what was going on because I knew she'd call me "co-dependent." She'd already taken to calling me "self-destructive," having recently adopted for herself a theory of mind revolving around self-sabotage. She interpreted everything through that lens. And through that lens, I was very self-destructive.

I took the Chinatown bus each way, four hours on the bus plus half an hour on the T and almost an hour on the subway. It was a lot of travel for a one-night stay, but I did not want to stay for more than one night no matter how much my grandmother begged me to. I've always been soothed by long drives and highways and trains, so the trip ended up being my favorite part about the experience. I wore dark sunglasses, a baseball hat, and huge headphones. I listened to music the entire time. If I was sad, I listened to Radiohead. If I was angry, I listened to Fiona Apple. If I was feeling slutty I listened to The Neptunes. Those were my three states.

While I was away at school, my grandfather had gotten even better at his silent treatments toward my grandmother. I felt bad for him. He never admitted he was sad, because if he was sad about this, then he had to be sad about everything, and how much sadness could one man take? But when I was home, something changed in him. He wanted to be close. He'd spend all weekend in my room. He climbed into my bed to talk, just to talk, and he positioned my body so that my head rested on his chest. He told me the story of my mother and father bringing me home from the hospital in pastel pink pajamas. "They had a matching pink blankie, too," he said, descending into tears. "It had baby bunnies on it." He was brimming with both anger and a boundaryless affection. I stayed still and said nothing, hopeful he'd keep telling stories about my parents. His sons were dead, each of them had taken a turn being my father, and now my grandfather, *their* father, wanted a closeness with me I couldn't quite articulate. It was my body, but they were his sons.

My grandmother pushed me to say something to make him get sober, lift his head up higher, to show again the kind of blind ambition and faith that had carried him through so many years. But his affection lasted only as long as I remained silent. The moment I opened my mouth, asking leadingly whether he thought it might be a good idea to come home right after work so that my grandmother did not worry, he would spit at me, "Now you disrespect me, too?" and storm out of the house.

My grandmother saw me off in Chinatown each Sunday night, sending me back to school with kimbap and wakame from a shop off Mott Street. My grandparents loved Chinatown. They were on teasing terms with the cashiers at a little bakery where they got sweet coffee and melon-flavored bread. I spent a lot of time in Chinatown as a kid. Whenever we wanted to go on an outing as a family, that's where we went. We were a very big seafood family, and my grandpa had friends at the various fish markets. It's where I discovered he knew how to speak English just fine. I was on my BlackBerry while he was doing his thing in front of the big red sea bass on ice when I started making out parts of the conversation. To my surprise, he was speaking in English. For *years* he had made me translate for him at the doctor, the bank, the DMV, and it turns out he could speak English this whole time? The fish-monger spoke a similar English. Whimsically conjugated English, but American English it undeniably was. Immigrant English, a dialect all their own. Gloria Anzaldúa said that when the Third World and the First World meet, they rub against each other and produce an open wound. Chinatown, though. It was a pretty sight.

As the bus peeled out of New York, I felt overwhelmed by re-lief to be leaving them, and that relief gnawed at me. My grand-parents took me in, they gave me everything. But I felt nothing for them. I missed my parents, but I do not remember loving them. I might have loved my aunt and uncle as a child but I was so young, I do not remember. Feeling nothing for my family made me feel evil. Broken.

The Latine campus groups seemed to be full of people who loved their families. When they performed moving spoken-word poems about their ancestors and talked about their abuelas cook-ing or singing or sharing gems of wisdom, I found myself dis-associating and, like in a fever dream, all the abuelas melted together into one large, magnanimous superabuela that shared a room with Jesus in the sky and sat above us like a pancake. To many of my ancestors, I would have been just another little brown girl, forgotten on another continent, passed around from hand to hand. Imagine being born a goldfish.

I returned to my dorm late one Sunday night to find a yellow envelope leaning against my door. I opened it immediately and when I saw its contents I rushed into my room, double-checked the lock on the door, turned off the lights, and pulled down the shades. The envelope was filled with coca tea bags. *From NW.* He'd read my essay, the one Abél had not quite been impressed by, where I rambled about never having tried coca. After catching me reading it over one day at the Peabody front desk, Nathaniel had goaded me into letting him read it.

"What's so interesting?" he'd asked, leaning over the desk.

"No, not now," I said without looking up.

"Sorry—are you enthralling yourself with your own writing? I can see it says *Caddaleena Idderaldey* at the top."

"Jesus Christ," I said.

"Show me. Please, come on, I want to read your paper, too."

I pushed the paper toward him. He snatched it up, skimmed the first two pages, and then looked up at me, suddenly full of pizzazz. "Did I ever tell you the story of the old lady I met during research who must have been at least eighty years old who insisted right then and there that we chew coca together and I was like, Am I seriously doing drugs with an octogenarian? What is my life?"

Nathaniel had shown me his cards. Coca leaves are illegal in the United States. He—or his father—had broken laws I didn't even know existed because I was scared that learning laws about customs or the transportation of dry foodstuffs, or even googling how you transport anything internationally outside of using the Delgado Travel in Jackson Heights, would implicate me in the human trafficking ring I always suspected I had connection to, on some level I believed that everyone did. Like my grandmother, I had been socialized around a certain type of man. The strongman, the caudillo, the jefe, the elder, the don, the capo, the OG, the godfather, the Italian deli owner who has for the past fifteen years personally prepared the morning coffee preferred by highway workers and the early birds of the 83rd Precinct of the NYPD. People who knew people. Was this finally my turn? Would the small-town teenage beauty queen be getting flowers from the visiting drug lord? I felt burdened by a new power. I flushed the tea bags down the toilet while making the sign of the cross.

By then it was late in reading period—the precious fleeting week between the end of classes and the start of final exams. Like everyone else, I had tests to study for, essays to write, and all-nighters to pull and then brag about. But everything I put in my mouth made me dry heave. I lay motionless in bed, curled up like a hurt animal hiding its belly tenderful with organs. My stomach grumbled but I didn't have the energy to do anything about it. My skin took on a gray cast. I began to enjoy the weakness that comes from self-deprivation, falling in and out of consciousness felt good, *it was so me,* I finally looked how I felt. Now I'm awake, now I'm not. Now I remember. Now I forget. I am vertical. Now I am not. I am a rag doll. Henry? Henners? Mr. Kissinger, where did you go?

My grandmother's text messages harangued me in my fugue state. *Catalina, talk to him. Catalina, do something.*

I was sure I could do nothing.

She did not ask how I was doing. It occurred to me she didn't really ask me questions, in general. I sent all her calls to voicemail and spent every waking moment consumed by guilt over not listening to the messages. I knew her voice would be pained and pleading. It was nice of God to knock me unconscious now and then.

As if that wasn't enough traumarama, the DREAM Act wasn't leaving me alone, either. After the catastrophic midterm elections the previous month, Obama had pledged to introduce the DREAM Act in the House. It was a bold thing for a lame-duck session to undertake, but anyone who still cared, or still held hope, wanted to try one more time before the new Republican Congress stepped in. The bill was heading to the Senate sometime by the end of finals week. I was too tired to feel anything other than resentment that I had to feel something about it.

The only responsibility I could handle was my shift at the Peabody. It felt extremely right to cry in there. The working class has always felt the simultaneous warmth and chill of the church when we visit museums and I was never able to shake it. The first floor was dedicated to Native Americans, and as soon as I opened the doors to that room, music washed over me. Drums, tribal chanting, sounds from the Plains. They had a tobacco pipe they believe belonged to Sitting Bull and drawings of warriors in battle astride horses. I cried in the Oceania room and the Mexico and Central America rooms and I cried among the Fijian war clubs and headdresses from Papua New Guinea. What other space could contain me?

I wasn't worried about finals. I'd get by. Even for the classes in which I hadn't participated all semester, where I sat in the back of the class with a hoodie pulled over my head, I had still done my readings. I'd still been listening.

I was listening in Abél's seminar when he talked about the Shining Path and how brutally they hurt campesinas in the highlands. He said that women and girls prepared for the guerrillas and paramilitaries by putting potatoes up their vaginas to avoid rape, or maybe to avoid getting pregnant if they were raped. One reliable fact about gaggles of men is their method of camaraderie building, a spot of rape to soothe the nerves or distract them from a lack of organizational forethought. They redraw maps into the night in White Nights cosplay, thinking up brilliant new constitutions for the republic on the way to the bathroom. And they rape.

I was listening in English 341: The Postmodern Novel when we spent two weeks studying the campus novel, a genre that gained traction in the 1950s and explored tenure-track malaise and the existential crises of professors and students on campuses primarily in New England. The main attraction is the sex. Here are titles of the books in Philip Roth's David Kepesh trilogy: *The Breast, The Professor of Desire, The Dying Animal. The Dying Animal* was my favorite. The novel's protagonist, a literature professor, describes his young Cuban American student (he's already described her "gorgeous breasts") in this way: "She thinks, I'm telling him who I am. He's interested in who I am. That is true, but I am curious about who she is because I want to fuck her. I don't need all of this great interest in Kafka and Velázquez. Having this conversation with her, I am thinking, How much more am I going to have to go through? Three hours? Four? Will I go as far as eight hours? Twenty minutes into the veiling and already I'm wondering, what does any of this have to do with her skin and how she carries herself?"

So I learned that!

The only class I wasn't so sure about was my thesis colloquium with Sandoval. I still hadn't decided on a topic. Without a topic, there could be no outline, no bibliography. I wasn't even opening her emails. Maybe they were pleading, maybe they were mad, maybe if I waited long enough they'd stop and she'd forget about me. I was sure Nathaniel opened every email from his thesis advisor. Delphine did, too.

Among the artsy kids and the nerds there was much speculation about who would win the thesis prizes, the Hoopes Prizes. The English Department had lots of contenders. That year, there were ten theses on David Foster Wallace in the Signet *alone*. The honest-to-god truth is that even though I had not worked on my thesis at all, and even though I didn't even have a topic, I was 70 percent sure I would win a thesis prize. Why not? It was a stretch, but so was everything.

Delphine was definitely going to win a thesis prize. She helped discover some tiny protein mutation or something on a fruit fly and authored a paper for a science journal with her professor. She knew that I was blowing off Professor Sandoval and she insisted on getting a coffee to talk about it. I bristled at the suggestion. I felt like I was getting in trouble, which has always made me spiral.

We both ordered spicy Mexican hot chocolates at Simon's, a coffee shop right off the Quad.

"I love you very much," she began, her hand on mine. "And I'm telling you this because I love you. You're a hot mess right now, and I love that about you, but you need to graduate. Right?"

My eyes welled up with tears and I gulped down very hot hot chocolate.

"You're right," I said, doing my best to keep from crying and trying to recall the script. "I'll make an appointment with mental health and with the study center. I just need someone to talk to, to discuss time management techniques. I really appreciate your concern, I do feel loved, thank you."

She laughed. "Good, babe. Thank god for financial aid."

I aced the two finals I took. I missed Abél's in-class test worth 30 percent of my grade because I overslept. I didn't hear my alarm clock. I missed it entirely. When I arrived, students were leaving the building and handing back blue books at the door. I could be such a dipshit. I ran away, worried Abél would see me. What could I possibly say? And what could it possibly matter.

The next day, a Saturday, the DREAM Act once again failed to break the filibuster in the Senate. We were just five votes short of the sixty needed to advance the bill. The vote basically took place along party lines but there were a few extra cowardly Democrats who shifted course and joined their Republican colleagues. When I heard the news, I ran to the bathroom to throw up. I wasn't completely heartbroken because I knew it was going to happen and anticipating it took away some of the sting. All I felt was a terrible, sinking dread. My body did not want to carry the weight of me any longer.

The Signet had its annual holiday dinner that very night. The Signet party advertised itself as a night of debauchery with one bottle of champagne allotted to each person. I loved the holidays. I decided that nothing bad could happen to me at Christmastime. Tinsel and peppermint candy, paper snowflakes and real-ass snow, tuning into NY1 News at 5:00 A.M., hoping for a snow day from Mayor Bloomberg. If something magical was going to happen to me, ever, it was probably going to happen in December. I planned on wearing a vintage long-sleeved black backless dress from Halston, the pièce de résistance of my grandma's Goodwill collection. It was two sizes too small but it made me feel like a movie star.

I asked Nathaniel to be my date. He was going to end up at the Signet as one stop among many as part of his Saturday night party-hopping. Inviting him made me feel like he was coming to see me. Plus, the dress code was black tie and he definitely had that shit in his closet. As for me, I had my little black dress.

When I was blow-drying my hair, the dress ripped at the shoulder; the sleeve was still held up, but precariously.

I texted Nathaniel to ask him to bring a sewing kit.

"A sewing kit?"

"Yes, can you drop by the CVS to pick up a tiny sewing kit? I'll pay you back."

"Why do you need a sewing kit?"

Dress mishap.

Kyle ran to greet me at the door and we hugged each other for a long time. I hung up my coat.

"Let me borrow her for a minute," Kyle said to no one in particular, and pulled me into the kitchen.

"Look what I found," he crooned. He showed me a platter of burnt cinnamon buns in the fridge.

As the night went on, we all got sloppy. Still, no matter how much I drank, I was never drunk enough to fully buy into the premise that we were young and carefree and needed to leave it all on the dance floor. Around two in the morning, I sat down at the German piano in the corner of the room. I didn't have to pose. Everything around us was already posing, the chairs, the wallpaper, the teacups, the framed letters from Leonard Bernstein. Nathaniel arrived late and joined me at the piano. He lit a cigarette. I was surprised to see him smoke indoors but I didn't show surprise and I didn't say anything because no one else showed surprise and they didn't say anything. We sat in silence. He took a small sewing kit out of his pocket and placed it on the music stand in front of me. He wrapped his hand around mine. I told him I wanted to lie down on top of the piano. I was not capable of non-suggestive syntax or delivery. Maybe it was my mouth. My grandfather always said I looked like I had a filthy mouth. Nathaniel looked like he liked that idea, so I left him at the piano and took the sewing kit with me. I went to find Kyle.

I found him still in the kitchen and joined him on the cold floor, both of us leaning against the refrigerator to protect it with our bodies since he had also discovered old fudge and did not want to share it. I passed him the sewing kit and pointed to my torn dress.

"Please?" I asked. "I'm drunk."

"I'm drunk, too," he said, happily.

He put his head on my shoulder and sighed deeply.

"Look, Catalina, you're just sensitive. That's not a bad thing. All you need to do is learn to rein in your emotions and make them work for you; they work for you, you don't work for them."

He straightened up and removed the needle from the sewing kit. He brought it up to his eye, squinting hard, as if there was any chance of him threading that needle. I took the needle away from him and put it back in its little box.

"The minute I do that is the minute I destroy my sensibilities as a writer," I said.

"Well, I am an artist, too. And in my opinion, artists don't need to have a life of great suffering in order to make art, not necessarily anyway. I would even venture to say most artists have *not* lived lives of incredible suffering."

"I'm talking about the human condition."

"Do you believe in forced migration?"

"I don't know what that means."

The music felt louder than ever. I glimpsed Nathaniel in the hallway.

"What?"

"I said, I don't know what that means."

"Some people say that the transatlantic slave trade was an instance of migration and that African Americans are immigrants, too."

"Oh, no, that sounds stupid."

"Good."

The former American president's granddaughter was doing

the rounds with a disposable camera taking photos. With some difficulty, I got up off the floor and walked over to Nathaniel with my eyes dead on him. I'd never waited this long for something I wanted. I reached up, cusped Nathaniel's face, and kissed him for a long time until I tasted blood in my mouth and felt his chivalrous hold around my arm tighten into an impolite grip. The former American president's granddaughter laughed delightedly, her ponytail bobbing up and down. I don't know if she remembered me but we were in the same freshman seminar on Jane Austen. I had tried to impress her all semester. She hadn't looked up from her computer once.

She disappeared, and when she returned she was holding a can of whipped cream. "Can I eat raspberries with whipped cream off your breasts?" she asked loudly.

"Ordinarily, but I ate all my raspberries," I told her. She pouted.

"You also drank all your champagne. Ordinarily," Nathaniel said. "Look at you."

"What?"

"You are a silly little girl, Catalina," he said wearily. He kissed the top of my head and left the room. Maybe he left the party.

At some point I tucked myself into the couch for a little shut-eye. Despite my best intentions, I was unable to make it to the toilet when the vomiting began. People were throwing up everywhere. Jimmy in the sink. Alex on the flower beds up front. I threw up on the couch and covered it with someone's leopard print throw. Then I got the hell out of there.

I didn't feel safe getting inside a taxi and I couldn't think straight enough to figure out the shuttle to the Quad so I walked home. It was cold—the cold feels colder in New England, the dark looks darker. It's personal. I wasn't the only drunk girl stammering around with heels in her hand and no coat. I passed by

Quincy House and saw that a party had spilled over into the courtyard after being shut down by campus police.

I heard a boy loudly ask an officer, "Excuse me, sir, where is my drink?"

"We threw it away—*sir*."

"Why? It was just iced tea!"

"It definitely wasn't iced tea."

The boy pouted and admitted it wasn't just iced tea.

"Let's call a security escort to accompany you back to your dorm."

"Five more minutes," the boy said. "We want to rage."

I was walking barefoot on old Cambridge cobblestone, rust-colored and crumbling under blue lights, and images of older women janitors, aunties and titis and titas raced through my mind. I could practically see them on their knees, scrubbing off dried vomit around a toilet, permed hair in a tight bun. This is how it was at this place. I would be having a normal day, minding my damn business, and then fucking *Tía* comes out of nowhere with a shopping cart looking all nice with freckles on her cheeks and she warns you about chemtrails and the razors in the apples, saying you might want to remove your sleeve from the candle fire, nena watch out, pero nena do something, Francisco do some-thing. What could I do but take a fistful of NyQuil as soon as I stepped foot in my room?

PART THREE

Winter Break

I ONLY HAVE BEAUTIFUL childhood memories of December in the city—school field trips to watch *The Nutcracker* at Lincoln Center, sneering at tourists admiring the Rockefeller Center Christmas Tree but taking secret, furtive glances and loving it. We did not have a Christmas tree in our home, and we did not exchange presents, and my grandparents said *thank you* when someone said *Merry Christmas* but they didn't say it back. For Jehovah's Witnesses, Christmas is illicit; perhaps because of that, I passionately loved it. In my head I had a Christmas tree year-round, and it was artificial and white, with silver trimmings and white and silver ornaments. I had a Yule log crackling with fire and a green hand-knit stocking that said *Catalina* as well as a menorah and dreidels because the more the merrier, I loved Hanukkah, too. When people wished me a merry Christmas I always said it back and even took extra care to add *Happy Holidays* to be inclusive.

When we converted, my grandparents got rid of all idolatrous images in the home, including the gold cross necklace that they had given me for my First Communion in the second grade. They threw out just about everything, but once I opened one of my grandma's little boxes hidden in her underwear drawer and inside were a couple of solid gold crucifixes and a pendant of Mary and a silvery rosary, her secret cache of idols.

Converting was wonderful for my grandma. For the first time since she came to America, she had friends and family. Same for me. Believing in the Truth meant I could have aunts and uncles again. The congregation was made up of mostly Latin American immigrants. Most of them were lapsed Catholics and, though many were hard-liners and wished to adhere to a literal interpretation of the Bible, others were surprisingly liberal on issues like education and abortion. Quietly, of course. Very quietly. Many of them were immigrants from Honduras, the Dominican Republic, Haiti, Venezuela, Colombia, and Chile, they had seen dictatorships and disappearances, and if freedom meant living in Sodom, they were more than willing to set up house.

Some religions are famous for ostracizing defectors. The Witnesses are notorious for this, but my grandparents did not stop talking to me when I left; in fact, they did not seem surprised at all when I sat them down after my first year of college and told them that I was not going to go to meetings anymore. They didn't even try to change my mind. Not once. I was almost a little hurt by how well they handled it. It felt like they never thought I was going to stay—something about me tipped them off early that I was not part of God's chosen people and belonged elsewhere, in what they called "the World." I was also relieved. Even though he could be deeply misogynist, and a machista, and a narcissistic know-it-all, my grandfather showed admiration every time I said no to him. He found my behavior outrageous, even despicable, but he admired the nerve.

Christmas came and went in our home without any notice.

Harvard gave us five weeks off after the fall semester, ostensibly to pursue off-campus passions and personal interests best suited to our "individual situations," which meant some people went to France and some people did internships and the rest of us scrambled for something to do in our hometowns and fought with our parents. They closed all the dining halls and turned off our card access to the dorms. Some people applied to stay on campus but not many were allowed to. We called it "J-term." Administrators called it "the January Experience."

As part of his January Experience, Nathaniel was in the remote highlands of Peru with Dr. Murphy, conducting ethnographic interviews and oral histories, collecting local stories that might lead them to the great Rosetta stone khipu. Some of these villages had continued to use khipus long after the Spanish came. After a few weeks of that he'd unwind in Santa Marta, Colombia, "working" on a side project about stringed forms of expression in the Andes post-conquest. Nathaniel wanted to look at how embodied knowledge is passed down among the brown and Black people who made stringed instruments the way their fathers and grandfathers did. He didn't even invite me. Of course, there was no way for me to leave the country and I knew that. But *he* didn't know I couldn't leave the country. He just didn't invite me.

When he was in Santa Marta, Nathaniel posted a lot of beautiful photos on Facebook—of beaches, street vendors and their wares, bananas, coconuts, and mangoes. In the summer, I liked to eat one mango a day, thirty-one mangoes a month, although mango snobs might scoff at the nomenclature since they came from the Foodtown in Bushwick. (I had never had a mango from the Mango Belt; ergo, I had never really had a mango.) Like the other Facebook photo albums dedicated to his travels, this one was titled something in Spanish. *La tierra del olvido*. In his hands, Spanish had the aesthetic appeal of raw chicken, the liminal mon-

strosity stuck between a frightened animal and a date-night roast
chicken.

As for me, I was spending J-term in Queens, sandwiched between my grieving grandparents. They both seemed so frail and
so sad. My grandma was relieved to have me home, but the five
weeks before me felt interminable. New Year's came and went as
quietly as Christmas.

It was the snowiest winter in New York City I'd ever lived
through. Blizzard after blizzard. My grandfather's construction
jobs were often shut down because of the snow and ice, and when
they weren't, he thanked God for the work and did not complain
about his frozen toes and fingers, split and bleeding, and he did
not complain when the equipment stopped working in the cold.
Work was work. For stretches of time, the three of us were
cooped up in the house hibernating, watching movies, driving
each other crazy.

One evening, we were in the middle of watching *Terminator 2:
Judgment Day* when my grandfather received a call letting him
know not to bother coming to work in the morning. The construction site was still coated in ice and buried deep in snow, and
the boss didn't want a personal injury nightmare on his hands.
But another day without work also meant another day without
pay. We finished the movie in silence. It was hard to get up from
the couch and move on to the next activity because I was certain
he would yell if we left the room, he would claim we were heart-
less bitches who didn't care if he lived or died. My grandmother
and I exchanged a look. I reached for my computer. She brought
out a baby-pink mani-pedi set and began to do her nails.

My grandfather shot her a disgusted look and finally spoke.

"No woman who actually loved her husband would file her feet
in front of him because it would matter to her that when he thinks
of her, he thinks of a woman and not a teenage boy."

"You know, human bodies aren't hot all the time," I said.

"Ah, who shows up but the genius from Harvard here to teach me about feminism?" He turned to me, his face flashing bright with an insult he really liked. "You talk like a prosecutor," he said with a mean smile. "Little Miss Prosecutor on her way to international court. Stop lazing around on the Internet, do something constructive with your time. Let's play chess."

For as long as I lived with them, my grandparents displayed one chessboard or another in the living room of the apartment. Chess reminded them that they were civilized no matter what other people said. They liked showy chessboards, antique ones or especially beautiful hand-carved ones they found at estate sales in Forest Hills. My grandfather taught me to play chess. He said he was very good at it. I wouldn't know. I was not very good.

"Which is the more important piece, the queen or a pawn?"

"I can't give you a good answer because I need to concentrate right now," I said.

"This should be a very easy move. Focus."

"I am focusing."

A fascinating pedagogical technique my grandfather employed involved teaching me new rules by springing them on me in the middle of a game, waiting until I questioned one of his moves, and then Aha!-ing me with a lecture on the en passant rule or whatever. I couldn't shake the suspicion, when he taught me some new exception to the movement of pawns, that he was making all of the rules up as we went along in a deliberate effort to fuck with my head, or rather to sabotage me. If I ever wanted to play chess against literally anyone other than him, I risked making a fool of myself. Just imagine: I am playing chess against an American with an uneventful childhood on a patio in Paris. I look beautiful, my hair blows in the wind, and I move my pieces confidently. The happy American informs me I made an illegal move.

No, I tell him, *it's an exception. Exception to what?* he says. *This is definitely not allowed.* I try another move. I try another one. He puts his hand on mine and looks at me with pity.

"Check," my grandfather said. "You're distracted."

Ugh. I was distracted.

I moved my queen with the reckless certainty of a skyfall, and I lost her early. My king was threatened and my tower could save him. Did I say tower? Sorry. I meant *rook.* I learned the rules in Spanish. The obvious next move would have been to kill his queen with my rook in one fell swoop, but to prolong the enmity between the monarchs, to prolong the *drama,* I moved my rook to merely block the queen's attack. I let her live. He moved his bishop. I switched my knight and rook.

"You can't move two pieces at once."

"Of course you can," I said coolly. "It's called castling."

"It's called what now?"

"I don't know, I watched a video about it on YouTube."

"I've never seen that before," he said. "I play pickup games with old Italians in the park, but you know all these special rules?"

"I don't know it, I watched a video about it. Why am I in trouble for this?"

"Who says you're in trouble? I can't have a conversation with anyone here without you acting like you're being attacked."

"I *am* being attacked!" I said. "Why is this even a thing? Why are we fighting over this? Oh my god."

"Oh my god, oh my god," he mocked me. "Do your fancy move."

"In response to your *proletariat* move? How can something related to chess be fancy? Chess *is* fancy."

"I think it's best if you both just take a moment to breathe, calm down, return to the game once you've cooled down."

"Stay out of this, Abuela."

"That mouth on you," he said, focusing his eyes on me angrily. "What did I say *now*?"

"Don't talk to your grandma like that. If I had talked to my mother like that, she would have slapped me across the face."

"Is that your parenting standard? Your mother abused you!"

"What did you say about my mother?" he screamed.

"I didn't say anything *about* her. I pointed out you're holding up corporal punishment as the gold standard and maybe that's because you were raised with that example so you act like it's normal, but that's not right. Why would she slap you? I would never let you slap me."

"Oh? You *let* me do things now, I see, I'll ask your permission before I do anything," he said. "Little Miss Macha knows all about parenting."

"Maybe I do! Maybe it's about time somebody does," I said.

My grandfather looked shocked for a moment, and then he swung at me melodramatically, stopping short of my face.

"Get out," he said.

I burst into tears. "How did this happen? This doesn't make sense."

He stormed out of the room.

"Grandma," I cried, "why is he like this?"

I went toward her and leaned in for a hug that she accepted but did not return.

"You're both wrong," she said. "Tal para cual. You're made for each other."

Their congregation met on Sunday mornings and on Tuesdays at 7:30 P.M. My grandmother primped for church like she was the Bride of Christ herself and it drove my grandfather crazy. "In ten minutes, I will be out that door, if you're ready, you're ready, if you're not, too bad," my grandfather warned as he breezed past me on his way to the bathroom.

"I'll be ready, worry about yourself because I'll be ready," my grandmother said, applying lipstick, her hair still wet. "Of course I wouldn't have to rush if you learned to use an *iron.*"

They went on like this until they were out the door together, at the ten-minute mark just as she'd promised. Her poor wet hair. The walk to the Kingdom Hall was twenty-five minutes. It was bitter, cold, and dark, and the streets were largely unplowed. When snowplows went out, Manhattan took preference, Park Slope got plowed before East New York, white Queens got plowed before brown Queens, etc. I was in a not-plowed area; people shoved the snow to the sides into impossible mountains you had to climb to cross the street.

When they left for their meeting, I put the kettle on for tea and got out my laptop. I had just discovered the Casual Encounters section on Craigslist. I had a secret email account associated with a secret phone number that I still blocked with *67 to call mean, older Manhattan men to have phone sex. Sometimes they got carried away and asked if they could send a car to pick me up, to take me to them. I blocked those. You can imagine their end of the conversation. A lot of tight little pussy this, dumb little whore that. They weren't exactly poets. But I was. Why, I could pull from all of Western civilization for references to describe my body. Who would deign to dwell by a roadside dandelion but the poets? Who would stop for me if not for them? It was almost plagiarism.

Men! Men men men men men men men. I knew what they were thinking. I had read Freud and Norman Mailer, Murakami and Díaz and Bellow and Nabokov Nabokov Nabokov and I was submerged in the world of indie rock so I was intimately familiar with the music catalog of Ryan Adams. I knew what I could aspire to in the eyes of a sensitive man. "Oh, Maria, Maria / She fell in love in East L.A. / To the sounds of the guitar / Played by Carlos Santana."

I contorted my body into famous poses. I described myself so *beautifully* and went off into tangents but they kept coming back. They became quite taken with this girl they thought I was, they couldn't help it, they really liked the story, and there was always so much more, like Scheherazade day by day. So I called them one by one and talked them through their journeys toward an orgasm and just as they were about to climax, I raised my voice a few octaves and said, *Hasta la vista, baby!*

Part of the problem is that my ability to achieve an orgasm did not depend on anyone else, or even on whether or not I was turned on. It was mechanical. Anyone could have me writhing on their floor because it wasn't about them. It was about me. I could have five or six orgasms and still be stunningly bored. After I came, I was ejected from Olympus and became fully human again. After all that hullabaloo, this was an orgasm. That was all, this was it. For a brief moment, the fruits of being a bad girl seemed paltry and small compared to the warmth and coziness I associated with being a good one.

It's demoralizing, the lack of good parts in this town for a girl like me. I wondered how much time various men might have spent with me in the Villa Grimaldi of their big brains and in what way. What embarrassing torture had I been put through? In their dreams, did I find them funny? Did they discover me? Did they teach me funny little German words? Did they imagine me expressing insatiety for their cock, men whose hometowns were not Liverpool or Sheffield, a stone's throw from their childhood friend and bandmate, but variations upon "about an hour away from the city"?

When I hung up I took a ravishingly hot shower and sat on the floor of the tub until the hot water ran out.

One night, Nathaniel called me shortly after my grandparents came home from their meeting, just before 11:00 P.M. My

grandpa began grumbling and ranting loudly, loud enough for
Nathaniel to hear.

"What kind of self-respecting woman takes phone calls at this
hour?" he bellowed. It wasn't a question.

I put my hand over the receiver and mouthed *Basta, ya!*

He didn't stop.

"She's young, Francisco. Don't you remember when you were
young?"

I grabbed the first coat I saw and walked toward the door, fully
intending to take the call outside the building, in the snow. But
they continued.

"I do remember when I was young, which is why I know my
daughter should not be—"

"Granddaughter," I interrupted hatefully over my shoulder,
still trying in vain to muffle the receiver.

"Oh my god, Catalina, what are you doing? Do you enjoy getting a rise out of him?"

I did not, no, he yelled all the time and I did not like being
yelled at. But fighting him felt like practice for whatever hero's
journey God had set aside for me in the future so I did it anyway.
I braced in the doorway for whatever came next.

"Let me tell you something," my grandmother said, in a treach-
erous, rare assist to my grandfather's goal. "When you came to us,
I had two fears: one, that you would become a drug addict, and
two, that you would fall in love with a man who treats you badly,
and if you let a man treat you like this now, what kind of message
are you sending?"

"Americans talk on the phone at eleven P.M. all the time."

"We live by the word of God, not the word of man," said my
grandmother.

"God doesn't care about this at all."

"Your smartass mouth is going to get you slapped," my grand-father warned.

The threat delivered and received, I went outside to speak to Nathaniel peacefully in the snow.

"Hello, Catalina," he said.

"Nathaniel," I said, my breath sharp and visible. "Where in the world are you and what are you doing?"

There was a long silence. Interference. "Sorry, what was that?"

"How are things? What are you up to?"

"Oh man, it's crazy here. I've been dying to tell you—did you know that Simón Bolívar died here? Right here in Santa Marta. There's a museum at the hacienda where he died, and they have original Oswaldo Guayasamín paintings in the permanent exhibit. Do you know him? Ecuadorian painter?" He paused. "I really wish you were here."

"Yeah, me too."

"They have a clock here that some general immediately stopped after Bolívar died. He stopped it three minutes and fifty-five seconds after Bolívar died."

I bounced up and down to keep warm. We needed to get off Bolívar.

"I had a dream about you," I said, lying.

"What did you dream about?"

"Your hands." I couldn't say it without laughing.

"Does that work on guys usually?"

"Usually. I'm running out of tricks."

"Good. I like you without the tricks."

"No, you don't. That's just something you have to say because it's decent."

"Catalina," Nathaniel said.

"Yeah?"

"Send me a picture."

"What kind of picture?"

"Any kind of picture. Every kind."

I smiled. I felt desired, the most beautiful feeling in the world.

"Do you want me to make it snow?"

"Where?"

"Where you are."

"No, but I do want you to make it rain." He laughed at his joke.

"No," I said emphatically. "Never, ever say that again. I have to go, Nathaniel."

Have you ever seen a moonflower? They only bloom at night. Mallarmé thought the perfect book was an unopened one, never cracked, its pages never cut, the world inside begging to be discovered, a true virgin land. When was the last time you were allowed to put your hands around a dead language?

When I went back upstairs, the apartment was quiet. They had gone to bed. I took to bed myself and pulled up the comforter to the top of my chin and through my headphones I listened to more songs I imagined might remind Nathaniel of me.

✳ •

My grandmother woke up one night in terrible tooth pain. My grandparents did not have insurance, and a private-practice dentist was prohibitive so they went to a local dentistry school where students provided treatment under the supervision of faculty. It was sliding scale. It was like being a model for Bumble and Bumble and getting bangs.

We called the program first thing in the morning and were lucky enough to get an appointment the same day, an emergency appointment. All three of us went. The waiting room was crowded. There were three or four older men waiting; they looked like veterans, and in my opinion they appeared to be Italian. Out of all the different ways there are to be white, being Italian is my favorite. We waited over an hour. I could feel my grandfather's anger and my grandmother's panic rising by the second. She was crying loudly in pain.

Finally, a young Puerto Rican student introduced herself as Lauren and brought my grandma in for X-rays. I followed to help with translation, though Lauren was doing her best. My grandma's screams were now just whimpers and she wept softly through the entire process.

"Aw, it's all done," Lauren said with a small, sympathetic smile. "You did amazing. I'll be right back with the X-rays. We'll take a look."

Lauren returned with an older man who I assumed to be her faculty supervisor.

"Fernanda, you've got a walloping impacted wisdom tooth back there. It's infected, and you'll need surgery."

"When? Can you please treat her today? Look at her," I pleaded.

"Unfortunately, we can't do that. Patients must fast before any surgery like this."

"She did fast. Again, just look at her, she couldn't eat or drink if she wanted to!"

Lauren paused to consider. Her supervisor nodded silent approval.

"If you can stick around, my colleagues will try to fit you in at the end of the day," Lauren said.

"Oh my god I want to hug you," I said. "Thank you so, so much."

"Thank you very very much," my grandmother said. She looked pale and moist.

Back in the waiting room, my grandfather looked wrecked. The three of us waited. It was dark outside, and through the window I could see it was beginning to snow.

Finally, a young man with intense blue eyes approached us. His name tag said RANDY. "Fernanda, we can see you now."

I spent my time in the waiting room on my BlackBerry, on an email thread with Kyle where we were playing Fuck, Marry, Kill. An hour in, I was stressing over the impossible choice before me—Clarence Thomas, Samuel Alito, and Antonin Scalia—when Randy returned with an update. "She fought like hell to not go under!" the dental assistant told me. "I was scared for my life for a second there!" I laughed but he did not laugh. My grandmother was four feet, eleven inches, and paper-thin. Nobody feared her. This was a joke. My grandfather stared at a fixed point on the pale gray floor.

Finally, my grandmother came out. She had incredible bruising to half of her face, far beyond the mouth. There was heavy bruising around her eyes and on her nose. It was pretty shocking.

"What happened to her?" I asked Randy.

"Bruising can happen during a procedure, it's normal," he said.

"Bruising like *that*?" I asked. "Can I talk to the surgeon?"

"He's seeing someone right now, but it just looks like that now. Try cold compresses and Tylenol every four hours, and if a fever develops, give us a call."

We walked out in silence. My grandfather was pissed but he didn't say anything. He could have asked for another nurse or insisted on the doctor or asked for a patient's advocate but he did not have the linguistic capability to make a case for anything in a room full of American citizen medical professionals. Besides, the doctors and nurses and students who worked there did not really believe they owed explanations of their schooling, wisdom, or expertise to people who so badly needed them in the first place, people who have been in this country for years and seemed unable or unwilling to absorb English, people who seemed extraordinarily good at finding every loophole in the law so that their children had access to school, their children had health insurance, free lunch at school. Not to mention medical malpractice lawsuits: It was impossible to make a real living as a surgeon with the constant threat of being hit with a lawsuit carried out naively by the patient and hungrily by the ambulance chasers. It is so sad to see vulnerable people used as political pawns, but everyone knows the immigration system is broken and until it is fixed they are costing us money by the second. Having compassion for them didn't mean you took orders from them, especially when they complained about your work when you were already doing them a goddamn favor.

I was emailing Kyle to ask whether he'd fuck, marry, or kill Bloomberg, Giuliani, or Cuomo, Sr., while we waited for the taxi I said I would pay for—my grandfather wanted us to take the bus home, which I flat out refused—when I suddenly felt my grandfather's hand strike the phone out of my hands, and when it landed on the floor, he stomped on it till the screen was smashed.

"What are you doing?!" I cried.

"Ever since you went to Boston you've been unrecognizable, you never have time for your grandmother, you never have time for your grandfather, the whole world is Harvard, Harvard, Harvard. I've been losing out on work coming here just to sit like a clown. Has that even crossed your mind? You could be wondering how stressed I must be, *My poor grandfather. Maybe I can give him a word of encouragement,* but instead you act like you are ashamed of us. Your face is stuck in your phone talking to whatever man or *men* that is more important than your family. I'm sorry I don't work in an office, I guess that's what it takes to earn your respect these days."

I burst into tears.

"When in hell have I ever, *ever* said I don't respect you? You're screaming at me like it's true and it's not true," I said, my voice rising quickly, becoming suddenly high and loud. "If you don't apologize to me for screaming at me like this I'm heading back to Boston right now," I pronounced. An empty threat. The dorms were still shut down for break. Still, I gathered myself as though I could.

"If you walk away, you won't have a grandfather anymore," he said. I glanced at my grandmother and decided to stay.

On the ride home I texted with Nathaniel through the smashed screen in spite of my grandfather's glares. The cabdriver was a gringo and I bet on my belief my grandfather wouldn't yell at me in front of a gringo. I tried relaying to Nathaniel a careful version of the fight, since I didn't want him to think any of this was *cultural*. This wasn't Latine *culture*. It was my grandfather. And he was a very complicated man.

The next morning, I awoke to an email from Jim Young, asking if I was still in New York, and if we could have a catch-up coffee before I returned to school. I kind of knew why he wanted to see me. I really, really wanted it to happen and at the same time I wanted to run away from having to deal with any of this, not now, I wasn't ready. I suspected he was going to offer me a job. There had been a couple of departures at the magazine, word is they wanted to hire internally, and former interns counted as internally.

We met at a French bakery in Midtown. When I interned for Jim, I scheduled his lunches with writers and agents here—it was near his office and it was extremely loud and bright and cluttered, which afforded people a semblance of privacy. Jim hated agents, and he never said a word to me about his writers, but I could hear him on the phone, since my desk was near his, and he spoke very softly to his writers, almost in whispers, and he said this to them, he said: *No.*

My heart jumped when I saw him wave me over to his table.

"Aren't you freezing?" he said, giving me a warm half-hug.

"My ears and nose are but nothing else. Oh! My fingers." I held out my hand, wrinkly yellow and red.

"Catch me up," he said, and motioned for the server.

I ordered hot chocolate. Jim ordered the same.

Seeing Jim made me think about famous writers and their famous editors. This was an entire genre of daydream in my head. After J. D. Salinger finished *Catcher in the Rye,* he is said to have driven to his editor William Maxwell's house to read it out loud to him on the porch. When *Playboy* hired Walter Lowe, Jr., the first Black editor in its history, one of the first things he did was reach out to James Baldwin to invite him to write for the magazine. And then of course Joan Didion and Bob Silvers, the storied editor of *The New York Review of Books.* Have you read her novel *Salvador*? It's a little clumsy, but I liked it. Joan Didion wrote about the civil wars in Central America for *The New York Review of Books* in the late '70s. She had no experience in war writing or in Latin America or in civil conflict. She was there because she was a terrific writer. Every writer's dream: Your editor sends you to cover a big flashy story based on nothing but your blinding talent.

"Catalina, do you have plans for after college?" he asked. "There's going to be an opening at the magazine pretty soon and your name has come up."

"I don't know what to say," I stammered. "I feel really honored you'd even think of me."

"But?"

"My plans for after graduation are . . . still being figured out."

"By whom?"

It was the perfect moment to tell him but the secret was glowing red like coal in my throat and it choked me.

"By me, obviously, but there's a lot I have to think about and I can't rush into anything. If the world ended today, I would say yes, yes, one hundred percent yes, but there's so much I have to think about right now."

"As you wish." He leaned back in his chair, eyeing me with curiosity.

I was gutted, and I was relieved. If I ignored this, it might go away. It's how my grandparents handled bills. They just didn't open the envelopes.

"I'm thinking of getting a tattoo," I said, trying to change the subject. I said the first outrageous thing that came to my head. "My first tattoo," I lied. He couldn't see my ankle.

"Oh, no," Jim said. "Don't do that."

"Hear me out," I started. "Do you know what an association copy is?"

He shook his head. "No, I don't. What is it?"

"Okay, so association copies are books that collectors obsess over because they are rare books that were owned by someone related to the book or author, so for example, I saw a copy of *Lolita* online that Nabokov gave to his good friend Graham Greene, and the inscription is 'To Graham Greene, yada yada yada,' and Nabokov drew a butterfly and next to it are the words *green swallowtail dancing waist-high*. That's a kind of butterfly, a swallowtail, and obviously Nabokov was a lepidopterist, and anyway, that's the tattoo."

"Which part?"

"The *inscription*, Jim. Please don't make me repeat it."

"I think that's a great idea for a first tattoo for someone, it just doesn't have to be you. I forget, are you writing a thesis?"

"Yes, technically," I said.

"On?"

"The truth is that my thesis feels like it's collapsing under the weight of its own ambitions."

"Is something going on at home, or—?"

"No, nothing is wrong at home," I said too quickly.

"Okay, so, I don't know what's going on," Jim said with Wisconsin in the vowels. "But I want you to know whatever it is, it can be helped. If you want someone to talk to, I am a good listener and a bad judge."

I lied about the direction of my subway stop so he wouldn't walk me there. I wanted to go opposite wherever he went. I wanted to be alone.

"Let me know if anything changes," he said, and squeezed my shoulder supportively.

I walked straight up Sixth Avenue and Broadway, my feet killing me in heels, following a mental map of landmarks—Madison Square Garden, the Garment District, the Macy's in Herald Square, Lincoln Center. On the West Side, Columbia, and the Episcopalian church Joan Didion went to, and, in Harlem, Bill Clinton's office.

I never cared much for Central Park. I mean, don't get me wrong, I'd give up my *life* for Central Park, I recognized its majesty and beauty and, you know, *proletariat vim.* I simply did not like nature. If anything, I found nature annoying. I did not enjoy walks in the woods. I did not enjoy hiking. I did not enjoy looking at foliage. I did not like watching it snow. I did not like sunsets. I did not like sunrises. I did not like the sight of a full moon. I did not like looking at the ocean. I did not like swimming in the sea. Except for red roses, I did not like flowers of any kind. I thought tulips looked like erect penises; in fact, I saw phallic resemblance in most flowers. I loved Manhattan, though. I finally stopped at the great steps of the American Museum of Natural History.

Going to the American Museum of Natural History as a local has always been a bit of a mindfuck. You cannot remove tourists from the experience because they are part of it. Watching busloads of white American children make their way through the

halls of annihilated peoples made me feel like I was on an amusement park ride in hell. Since 1873, the museum has acquired
over half a million objects from North and South America, Africa,
Asia, Europe, and the Pacific Islands. A lot of these objects have
had quite the journey to the museum, passing through the hands
of local gangs and big-time warlords, the United Fruit Company,
the Department of Agriculture, Mrs. Escobar's living room.

I spent the most time in the Hall of Americas. On the third
floor toward the back, past the Maya and Aztec exhibits, is the
Inca Empire's little corner of the museum. The Inca's deadly encounter with the Spanish took place in 1532, forty years after
Christopher Columbus sailed the ocean blue. The Spaniards
came for gold, and they found it. It was everywhere, apparently,
and it caused great enthusiasm among the men. So they kid-
napped the Inca king and demanded a ransom of all the gold in
the empire. Legend has it that the Inca people brought the con-
quistadors some of the gold but refused to surrender all of it,
dumping the remainder into the rivers. The Spaniards killed the
Inca king and they made the people watch. The Inca king was
believed to be a god, and the public spectacle of his murder
seemed designed to move things along. A people who saw their
god killed before them might not put up a fight for long. Many
people did fight, for many decades, but the Spanish empire
spread like an oil spill.

I left the Hall of Americas and headed downstairs to the
Roman wing. I shuddered in anger and awe. In *Ways of Seeing,*
John Berger says we treat some works of art like holy relics because they had to survive a lot to get to us. Art historians study the
provenance of the artwork to understand more fully the historical
context that produced the art, how many sticky hands it had to
go through, how many backs of trucks and warehouses and ship-
ping containers and nondescript plane rides, how many moments

of claustrophobia. Of course, determining provenance wasn't always possible because so much of it was looted. Anyway, the gold was here now, just like the khipu and just like me. We could have been anywhere in the world but tonight we were here, for you.

When Teddy Roosevelt was a Harvard freshman in 1876, he shot a fluffy white owl in Long Island. I found it in the Theodore Roosevelt Memorial Hall on the first floor, not far from the bronze statue of Roosevelt sitting on a bench. He collected wild things to keep in his bedroom, a section of which he called the *Teddy Roosevelt Natural History Museum.* This is how Teddy loved his animals: He killed them, stuffed them, then kept them to look at forever. "I would like to see all harmless wild things, but especially birds, protected in every way," he said. Okay. Imagine shooting a fucking plover.

The problem with being an object of beauty, a beautiful object, is that you exist only when you're looked at and thus to remain alive you must be constantly looked at, the way some sharks need to be in motion to breathe. It feels like soul death when their eyes are off you.

I went home and climbed into bed with my laptop, refreshing *Pink Is the New Blog* over and over until my grandmother allowed me to go to sleep. I was forbidden from going to bed before 9:00 P.M. Her face was still covered in swelling and bruises. I slept for fourteen hours. I woke up around 11:00 A.M. with a headache.

When faced by the enormous question mark that was my life after graduation, my grandparents retreated into a fantasy world where their golden grandchild would keep pulling herself up to ever greater heights by her tough, weathered bootstraps. But sleeping was my favorite coping strategy. Jim Young and impossible job offers couldn't reach me in my sleep. Drinking could have been another way to cope, but the problem with drinking is

that I threw up very quickly and I didn't want to die choking on
my own vomit, on my knees, on a toilet. So I just put myself to
bed.

The earlier the sun went down, the earlier I wanted to sleep. I
was good and ready to punch out for the day around five, and the
evenings were endless. I took a Benadryl and a NyQuil most
nights, and then one night I took more and more and even more.
I threw up violently. I sat on the floor with my hands over my
eyes, whimpering like a frightened calf, the room suddenly spin-
ning around me, lit bright laser blue.

Now my grandparents paid attention. Now they saw that I was
sad. My grandfather found me on the bathroom floor, and I said,
I need to lie down. I said, *Can you please not yell?* I said, *Can you
please not yell so much? Can you please not yell?* And they didn't.
For the rest of the week they didn't.

My grandmother tried to lure me away from the sadness with
a cupcake from Magnolia Bakery that she had forced my grumbling grandfather to pick up in Midtown. We shared a love of
sweets. My grandmother loved pies and scones and macaroons
and mousse and cheesecake and Italian flag cookies and even
fruitcake. I was partial to lip gloss that looked and smelled like
candy. It's how she handled me not wanting to go to school as a
kid, back when I did not know English and school was terrifying.
If I made it through the week, my grandmother made me cheese
and cane sugar empanadas or bought me a lip gloss from the
drugstore. The Magnolia cupcake did not work, I remained in
bed, eyes shut, my pillow wet with tears. So then she tried to
make me sancocho. My grandfather's suggestion that she make
me sancocho with supermarket chicken nearly killed her. Back
when there were henhouses in Brooklyn, she had a chicken killed
for me every time I caught a cold; these days, she went to the Polish butcher in Maspeth.

My grandfather, for his part, wanted me to think away the sadness. He got a bunch of pop science books from the library, read them, and communicated to me everything that I was doing wrong—my diet, my gut health, my posture, I didn't drink enough water, I didn't exercise or meditate, I either got too much or too little sleep. And I certainly was not getting enough vitamin D.

But I knew I just needed to nap. I just needed to lie down and close my eyes. I lay motionless on my stomach, my entire body vibrating with panic and inertia, until my grandmother approached me to say it was nine o'clock.

"See? Was that so bad?" she asked.

I levitated with relief.

When my grandparents saw me lying around like a log in the daytime, they took turns climbing into my bed. They spooned me and stroked my hair.

"How many days has it been since you washed your hair?"

"You need to start doing crunches."

"When are you getting your eyebrows threaded?"

I spent all my time in bed, alternating between watching *Breaking Bad* and crying. *Breaking Bad* was my favorite TV show but I had to read spoilers beforehand or I could not watch it. I watched with subtitles on, the volume low, and I fast-forwarded through the most violent parts. I didn't have a stomach for violence. I was, however, very interested in organized crime. I held on to hope that my parents, who were nobodies in the world of responsible citizens, might have been somebodies in the world of line cooks with prison tattoos. On occasion I've tried to embellish the story of who my parents were or how they died because the knowable facts about their deaths are so utterly boring as to be insulting. I think my dad was speeding, and neither he nor my mom was wearing a seatbelt. My grandparents told me there was no evidence that my father was intoxicated behind the wheel, but I simply did not trust Latin American death certificates. The Catholic Church has tried to deny a simple Christian burial to many people, cruelly, famously to people who take their own lives, so families are known to pay bribes to coroners to change the cause of death to something more publicly respectable. That's the worst part. I don't think there was any menacing intrigue or conspiracy or exchange of hush money in my parents' deaths. It was stupid. They were stupid kids barely out of their teens speeding and not wearing seatbelts with their baby in the back seat. They lived in the Third World and they had no plans to leave. My grandparents were the ones with dreams. Their dreams had not come true. Maybe my parents were smart to not have dreams. Maybe they did have dreams, but I just wouldn't find those dreams respectable. Maybe I'd cringe. Maybe my dad wanted to be a DJ.

* •

I found out about my grandfather's deportation order the way I all too often learned important things about my family, which is that I found an unopened envelope. This particular envelope was where it was supposed to be—in the rusted mailbox on the side of our building—but in my grandparents' apartment, in the kitchen, in the drawers below the sink, there was always a stack of unopened envelopes. There were envelopes from the gas company, the electric company, phone bills, mostly it was bills. We never got mail from people we knew, and we did not buy anything that would arrive to us through the mail, so anything that came in through the mailbox was a request or demand for money. It froze my grandparents into inaction. They eventually paid off all the bills, but it seemed to take the electricity shutting off for a weekend here and there.

My grandma, in an effort to force me to move my body even a little bit, had asked me to run down and get the mail. As I slowly climbed back up the stairs, admiring my own weakness, I flipped through the stack of mail and found an official-looking letter addressed to my grandfather from the United States Department of Justice, Executive Office for Immigration Review. My grandfather was at work. This couldn't wait. I sat down on the stairs and ripped the envelope open. It read: DECISION OF THE IMMIGRATION JUDGE: NOTICE OF AUTOMATIC REMOVAL.

At first, I was weirdly calm. I did not want to let "them" win, whoever "they" were. I carried myself like representatives of the white race were taking notes in the back of the room, eyes fixed on me should I make a mistake. I wasn't sad. They wanted me to be sad, and I would not do as I was told. I wasn't sad. I was crying, but I wasn't *sad*.

I refocused my eyes and read more:

JURISDICTION WAS ESTABLISHED IN THIS MATTER BY THE FILING OF A NOTICE TO APPEAR WITH THE EXECUTIVE OFFICE FOR IMMIGRATION REVIEW AND BY SERVICE UPON THE RESPONDENT. THE RESPONDENT WAS PROVIDED WRITTEN NOTICE OF THE TIME, DATE, AND LOCATION OF THE RESPONDENT'S REMOVAL HEARING. THE RESPONDENT FAILED TO APPEAR AT HIS HEARING AND EXCEPTIONAL CIRCUMSTANCES WERE NOT SHOWN FOR THIS FAILURE TO APPEAR. THIS HEARING WAS THEREFORE CONDUCTED IN ABSENTIA.

ORDER: THE RESPONDENT SHALL BE REMOVED TO ECUADOR BASED ON THE CHARGES CONTAINED IN THE NOTICE TO APPEAR.

Notice to Appear? In absentia? I thought about the drawer. I was already in a state, so I ran to the kitchen, opened the cabinet, and started looking. I made little piles from the mail, sorted according to size. Nothing.

I ran into the bathroom with the envelope. I closed the door and locked it, confusing for a moment the ice-cold amphetamine rush of fear with the high that something historic was happening to us. I didn't know what a deportation actually involved. I imagined an airplane suspended in the air full of brown and Black men in pink prison uniforms—a Sheriff Joe Arpaio original—and chains and handcuffs. Where would they be dropped off? I'd heard stories of migrants being driven across the border without money or papers or phones, dropped off defenseless in cartel-run areas. Let's say this happens to you. What would you do? Describe your plan below. I'm dying to know.

_____

_____

_____

_____

Then I went into my grandparents' bedroom and rushed to my grandfather's bedside table. I pulled the handle open so hard that the entire drawer came out. I caught it and knelt on the floor. I didn't want to look through my grandfather's personal belongings; I was repelled by the idea of what I might find. But there it was. An opened envelope containing a Hearing Notice from ICE, Immigration and Customs Enforcement, postmarked November 20. Tucked right below the envelope, folded into quarters, was a weathered slip of paper with NOTICE TO APPEAR written at the top, also from ICE, dated October 1.

Dios mío por favor. I couldn't get the words out. So I screamed. My grandmother ran into the room in a panic, asking what was wrong.

"I'll be right back," I told her. "Please, you stay here. Don't . . . open the door to anyone."

Out on the street, I called my grandfather. He didn't pick up the first time, or the second time, but on the third time he did.

He began to cry, too. He was sad. He didn't yell. He said something about an ICE raid at one of his construction jobs back in the fall, they were looking for someone else, but instead picked up my grandfather and some of the other guys as collateral arrests. ICE let them all go, but not without initiating their deportation proceedings.

Abuelo, I can help. I can fix this, I can help, I will not let this happen.

I don't really remember the rest.

It was hard to believe something this exciting was happening to us. Not in a good way. In fact, it was the worst possible scenario coming true. But the violence in our lives was an accumulation of many indignities over time. Except for the colorful indignities, our lives were dull. This would actually move the plot along. Something primal kicked in. I had myself. I realized I'd been training my whole life for this moment. The energy I had for so long attributed to the Dreamers arrived upon me like the holy dove. This required a to-do list. I believed talking to any senator was possible, I believed the right words could soften any heart, I knew the right email sent to the right person's boss could reverse anything short of death, and maybe even death.

I was overcome by a great love for my grandfather. Despite his faults, he was the man who raised me. If anyone hurt me, he would kill them, and anticipating it, fearing it, wondering how it would feel, was part of the life-sustaining chaos of our home. Even the elders knew to mind their manners when it came to me. My grandfather made it clear that I was not under their jurisdiction.

When I was in the tenth grade, I made the mistake of burning a White Stripes CD for an elder's son. His mom found the CD in his room, under his bed, with the terrifying title—*Get Behind Me Satan*—in my handwriting. The elder took me aside the next time he saw me at the Kingdom Hall.

"What kind of music are you listening to, Catalina?" he scolded.

"I can explain," I said, unsure of how to spin it but confident I could.

He gave me a look. I told him Jack White grew up very religious and the Bible was his favorite book and one of his chief inspirations; in fact the title of the album referred to something Jesus said to Peter in the book of Matthew.

The elder studied my face, which was paused at the perfect frame, a good girl smile.

"Just keep it to yourself," he said. "Okay?"

"Okay," I said.

But it was not okay. My grandfather was outraged when he heard another man had tried to parent me; in fact, another man had tried to *discipline* me. He didn't care about the CD. It was the principle of the matter. At the next meeting, I saw my grandfather make a beeline to the strict but kindly elder with his chest puffed out and his face in a snarl. His voice projected. From a few rows away I could hear him perfectly.

"I heard you had something to say to my granddaughter," he said to the elder.

I put my hand over my mouth.

"If you have anything to say to her, you go through me. Is that clear?"

The elder blanched at the overreaction and my grandfather smiled and offered his hand for a handshake. I remember everything about that moment.

In the fifth grade, I was assigned to make a model of the Manhattan Bridge. We were learning state history for a test and we all got different bridges. I was so jealous of the kids who got the Brooklyn Bridge. My grandfather took over. He went to Home Depot and spent all night whistling and working on a model of the Manhattan Bridge. When I woke up, there it was, on the table, built by elves overnight. I was so proud of being related to this man who could make anything, fix anything, build anything, deconstruct anything, survive anything. My grandfather was a genius.

That night I looked for articles about Dreamers or parents of Dreamers fighting their deportation orders and wrote down the names of all the lawyers consulted. I found their email addresses and wrote them one by one asking for a call. The first lawyer who wrote me back offered to meet the next afternoon. He said, *Why don't you just drop by?*

I was surprised that the address he gave me belonged to a Catholic church on the Lower East Side. He told me I could find him in the basement.

"Call me Josh," he said, greeting me with a firm handshake.

"What do you do here?" I asked.

The place was run by nuns and it provided services to immigrant communities in the Lower East Side. "I'm here pro bono, but they don't even need me. If they took the bar *today* they'd pass, especially Sister Naomi."

An old lady I took to be Sister Naomi smiled big. I felt like I could trust the man. Josh. We sat down at a plastic foldout table and I told him what I knew, passing him the removal order from the Department of Justice along with the other papers from ICE that I'd found in my grandfather's drawer.

"What would you do?" I asked. "If you were in my situation, what would you do?"

"It's not good, Catalina," he said. "The best time to get an immigration lawyer would have been months ago, after ICE detained your grandfather and handed him that very first Notice to Appear, back in October. Any good immigration lawyer would have helped you to devise a plan to defend against removal. Depending on the details of your grandfather's history, they might have been able to request what we call a Merit Hearing. Maybe even make the case for an adjustment of status, or at least what we call a 'stay'—which is basically more time to build a case or appeal."

"But now? Can an in absentia order be stopped?"

"Removals in absentia, those are final orders. There's very little relief. They really don't like people who are no-shows. What you'd need to do is fight to reopen the case to win a second hearing. It's called a Motion to Reopen Removal Proceedings, and they aren't easy to get. It comes down to a discretionary choice made by the immigration judge whether or not to offer relief."

I wrote down everything Josh told me, as fast as I could.

"We need that," I said. "How do we do it?"

"Well, your grandfather, he'd have to make a convincing case explaining why he did not appear in court. Maybe he never received the notice? Maybe it was sent to the wrong address? Maybe, through some exceptional circumstance such as travel or illness, he was unable to appear at his hearing?"

I looked down, unable to meet Josh's inquiring gaze. Silence lingered between us.

"Here's the good news, Catalina," he said, with a fresh attitude. "If you were to find an immigration lawyer to help you file that motion to reopen, the court would have to grant a temporary automatic stay of the removal order, which would remain in effect for however long it took for an immigration judge to make a decision."

"Automatically?" I asked.

"Automatically," Josh said, leaning back with a sigh. "That might give your family some time to think things through. And, I should add, good press is usually not a bad idea. If people know who you are, if they know you're their neighbor, their friend, their student, their patient . . . Well, it's a gamble, but if you make it troublesome for ICE to focus on you, maybe they'll think it's more trouble than it's worth and go after easier prey or bigger prey. Filing a motion to reopen could buy you some time to make some noise."

"Okay. Yes, I'll do that," I said.

"Catalina, you need help. I'm a lawyer. These nuns are basically lawyers. Tell your grandfather to come by as soon as possible, and we'll get to work."

I said goodbye to my new friends, lawyer Josh and Sister Naomi, and walked around the Lower East Side until dark. I wanted to be alone. I got an iced coffee despite the cold and walked around until I found a bright head shop full of *stuff*. Bright, discordantly patterned tchotchkes hung from every corner. There were rosaries, saint medallions, Tibetan prayer flags, incense, Day of the Dead decorations. I felt a rush of objectless patriotism and redirected it toward myself. I stopped by every mirror I saw, every reflective surface. I almost didn't recognize myself, for the self of the mind is always, or usually, a summer self, and in my mind I was very tan, but in the mirror I looked almost blue. It didn't look like me. It wasn't me, but I felt a lot of tenderness toward that girl, that sad, pale little thing. I hoped she had a good support system.

I spotted a verbena perfume oil and bought it instantly. For as long as I knew him, my grandfather bathed himself in it. He started wearing it in military school. Manuelita Sáenz herself, the

Ecuadorian lover of Simón Bolívar, the great liberator, was partial to verbena cologne, as it was the fragrance used by the revolutionary men who surrounded her. I read this in García Márquez, the source of all my knowledge of Simón Bolívar, aside from, of course, my grandfather, despite what Nathaniel might have imagined about himself. I had long cast Bolívar in my head as Alejandro Sanz on horseback.

Back at home, I put on the kettle for tea and crawled into bed with my computer. *Good press is usually not a bad idea.* I logged in to my Harvard email and typed in A. Everyone with a prominent A in their name came up. I did this from A to Z, scanning the names that popped up for the most important person I knew, anyone who could influence the case. Then it hit me. *Byron Wheeler.* Byron Wheeler was the most famous person I knew. I asked Nathaniel for his dad's email. I told him I needed advice about my postgrad plans and he was all, *Of course of course, talk to my dad.*

I fussed around with a new email signature. Putting Harvard next to your name reminds the world that you are committing four years to being socialized at the institutionest of institutions. You'll be fine being told what to do.

Catalina Ituralde
Harvard College
Class of 2011

To: Byron Wheeler
From: Catalina Ituralde
Subject: Talk
8:47 P.M.

Hi, Mr. Wheeler, I have a sensitive subject to discuss with you. It's not a conversation I can have over email. Do you have any time to talk? Whenever it is most convenient for you. Absolutely no worries if you're too busy or don't want to, a no is fine and I don't need an explanation.

To: Catalina Ituralde
From: Byron Wheeler
Re: Talk
8:52 P.M.

213-342-8745

BW

We had a back-and-forth for a bit because we disagreed on mode of communication. He insisted on the telephone, and I re- fused it. I found extemporaneous conversation on the phone physically sickening. We agreed, as a compromise, to meet for coffee the following morning at LPQ on Twenty-eighth Street. He was drinking a cappuccino when I got there five minutes early. I was going to run away to the bathroom so I could arrive at exactly 11:30 A.M. as we had agreed, but Byron spotted me and stood up to greet me.

Oscar nominations would be announced later in January and Byron Wheeler was in the middle of his award-season campaign- ing. It was very nice of him to give me the time. He had spent the past three years healing—after he had a ministroke he stopped smoking, began to exercise every day. He meditated. This was widely believed to be his year.

"How can I be of service?" Byron asked.

"What do you know about illegal immigrants?" I asked. "Do you know anyone personally?"

"Not enough, and I am sure I do. Why do you ask?"

"You definitely know at least one." I pointed both thumbs at myself.

Byron leaned forward and lowered his voice.

"Are you serious? Is everything all right?"

"Yes. I mean, I am serious. Have you heard about the Dreamers? It's kids whose parents or whoever made the decision to bring them here as children. You're still undocumented if you're a Dreamer, you're just probably less likely to be deported because then there's outcry, you know? Like, if I got deported, people would care, I think, I hope, because of Harvard, which isn't fair but it is what it is. That is hard enough, but then I found out my grandfather was ignoring a deportation order he was sent earlier this year."

"Have you spoken to a lawyer?"

"Yes, he'll handle some . . . paperwork. But he said to gather support for my grandpa's case."

"Thank you so much for confiding in me," he said. "Is there really truly no way out of this? Harvard can't get involved and get you a visa?"

"That wouldn't help my grandfather, but no. For me it's marriage or legislation, that's it, that's literally it."

"Marriage?"

"Citizens can petition for their spouses to receive green cards."

"So there *is* a solution."

"No. That's not something I'm ever going to do."

"You can marry Nathaniel," he said breezily.

I blushed despite myself. "Nathaniel doesn't even know. And . . . also doesn't help my grandfather."

"You shouldn't have to worry about this," he said sincerely. "It's such a shame. You have such a bright future ahead of you. You've been through a lot, but you're a fighter. You'll come out the other end stronger. I want to help however I can."

"That's really kind of you. Thank you."

"How about this?" he said, thinking out loud. "An eight-, nine-minute documentary short about your last days at Harvard. The sadness, the joy, the grief, the mourning, but also the excitement and the parties and the whole thing. It wouldn't be political, it'll be art. Or it'll be both, but we're showing the human side of all of this. They can judge for themselves. I think more than a couple of places would be happy to run it. PBS, HBO maybe, whatever you want."

"But I think I should highlight my grandfather's case, no?"

"Look, I'm sure your grandfather is a great man and I'm sure he's interesting and charming and all the rest, but it's your story that people will respond to. *You're* also undocumented, and it's *your* grandfather who is getting deported. *Dreamer risks losing it all.*"

"I don't think I have it in me to be a poster child."

"You'd make a wonderful poster child."

"I want to sell out and work for a hedge fund like everybody else."

"A hedge fund?" he laughed incredulously. "No, you don't."

"Not *now*, but in a world where I was good at math and science, I would sell my soul to the highest bidder for sure."

"You're just being provocative. You could never work for a hedge fund because you're not dead inside."

"Well, I think you're wrong."

"Why don't you think about it? I really think this is our best angle."

"Okay," I said. "I'll think about it."

"There you go," he said triumphantly. "You already have the dimples!"

I smiled.

Later that night, I emailed him.

To: Byron Wheeler
From: Catalina Ituralde
Subject: Coffee
11:39 P.M.

Hi, Mr. Wheeler—

Number one, I know you've asked me to call you Byron but it
feels so weird to call you Byron. You're a master in your field, I
don't want to assume a familiarity I will never feel because you
are Byron Wheeler. If I'm going to do anything public, I am more
than honored that you are the one I would be doing this with.
You're going to hate me for this, but I am still wondering if there
are other angles that we could take. I'm worried that focusing
on me and my private life might feel a little weird because my
childhood is confusing, even to me, and I don't want to pretend
we have this perfect little family.

To: Catalina Ituralde
From: B.W.
Subject: Re: Coffee
12:07 A.M.

completely understand ur apprehension. There are creative
ways around that, ways of framing a story where it's not dishon-
est. Rachel and I would love to have you over for dinner to discuss. Tomorrow? BW

＊ •

The Wheelers lived at 271 Columbus Avenue, a couple of blocks
away from the Met. The building's doorman led me to a decep-
tively busted elevator with gold doors and when they opened I

found myself inside the Wheelers' living room, which was bright white and enormous. I took great care to modulate my expression.

"Catalina, I've heard so much about you!" Rachel Wheeler cooed, coming toward me. I leaned in for a hug and we bumped heads. We laughed. Her resemblance to Nathaniel unnerved me, though I should have expected it. Somehow, with all of my attention on Byron, it hadn't even occurred to me that Nathaniel *had* a mother.

"I'm sorry, I'm a real big hugger," I said.

"No, I love that. Well, welcome! I've been hearing about you for ages."

From Nathaniel or Byron?

"Good things, I hope," I said.

"Oh, he thinks the world of you."

Still unclear.

"Wine, Catalina?"

"Yes, please."

"Rosé good?"

"Yes, thank you."

"This wine is actually from Peter and Maggie's wedding," Byron interjected. "We wanted to wait for a special occasion to open it and I can't think of a better time. Cheers."

We clinked glasses. No further explanation as to the identities of Peter and Maggie and I did not ask, but when I told Kyle this story, he suggested Maggie Gyllenhaal and Peter Sarsgaard.

For dinner, we had salmon cut into small square portions, the size of the smallest of the Watchtower tracts. There was a side of steamed broccoli. The salt was on the table.

"How do you like living in Boston, Catalina?" Mrs. Wheeler asked me.

"I love Boston, but nine out of ten times I just stay in my room and read."

"That's a shame. You must be working so hard all the time. Boston is a terrific city!"

"I've been to the JFK Museum, which is in Boston and has Hemingway's papers for some reason, and I've been to McLean. I don't know if that counts as a historical landmark." I laughed.

"What do you mean, McLean Hospital? Is it a landmark?"

"No. I was joking, though I do think to a certain kind of literary person it could be a landmark."

"You?" Byron interjected.

I felt shy. "That's where Sylvia Plath got the electroshock therapy she wrote about in *The Bell Jar* and Anne Sexton went there and so did Robert Lowell."

"So you're saying you have also gone to this hospital in Boston where all these depressed people have gone to get help?" Mrs. Wheeler asked seriously.

"No," I said, "not yet. For now it's just a landmark." It was time for a conversational pivot.

"Nobody knows this, but I really love New England. The Long Island shore, the WASPy poets, all of it."

"Who is your favorite New England poet?" Mrs. Wheeler asked.

"Probably Emily Dickinson."

"Did she die at that hospital, too?"

"I'm not sure how she died," I said, my heart sinking. Was this banter, or was she mad?

Mrs. Wheeler smiled warmly.

"I don't know much, Catalina, but if there is one piece of wisdom I can share with you, it's this: if you work your ass off, and you become rich, a room at the Mandarin Oriental is exactly the same thing as McLean, just with room service cocktails."

"Cheers to that," Byron said.

Over expensive unsalted salmon, Byron told the charming

Mrs. Wheeler about his, or our, documentary film idea. He had
clearly been thinking about it since we last met, and his convic-
tion had grown. Now he was animated, speaking of the injustices
faced by migrants, of the need to tell the stories of those hiding in
the shadows. Mrs. Wheeler nodded along approvingly, her eyes
checking in on me periodically. She was attentive, even tender.
Nathaniel was so lucky.

I was on cloud nine the entire subway ride home.

That night, I got into bed without washing my face and
searched around for the chocolate bar I left under my pillow in
case dinner with the Wheelers went poorly and I needed a pick-
me-up. I devoured it. In that moment, I would have done anything for that chocolate bar. *Hershey's. Hershey's of Hershey's
and the death squads.*

From: Catalina Ituralde
To: Byron Wheeler
Subject: [no subject]
12:01 A.M.

Let's do it.

PART FOUR

SPRING SEMESTER

LIFETIMES PASSED BY the time I returned to Cambridge. I never thought this day would come. I was graduating soon. Four years had once seemed eternal and here we were, at curtain call.

"Wait, just you wait," my grandfather told me. "You'll figure something out. You always do."

But there was nothing to figure out. I was frozen in fear and inertia. I lulled myself to sleep by rattling off to God all the reasons it would be mutually beneficial for me to not wake up in the morning, but when the son of a gun kept me alive I ragefully said, "Okay! You won!" and decided to approach my spring semester with an open mind, game for everything, memorizing as much as I could so I could revisit it all later when my life went to hell.

I took only three classes that semester: a required independent study thesis tutorial with Ruby Sandoval, Portuguese for Spanish Speakers, and Harvard's famous class on *Finnegans Wake*. I was taking only three classes because I had to make up for not doing any work on my thesis all year. I could have satisfied my foreign language requirement with any of my Latin American

Lit classes but I didn't want to be cheated out of learning a language. I suspected I had a secret talent for languages, English and Spanish had entered me by osmosis, and I wanted to uncover my true potential. Could I be a polyglot? Just two days of Introduction to Arabic made me run to the nearest Romance language. I had a loud and highly public antipathy to all things French and I was afraid of loving Italian too much, so I ended up taking Portuguese for Spanish Speakers, an accelerated Portuguese class that met every day and did not allow enrolled students to say Spanish words in a vaguely French way, a trick of the throat known as Portuñol.

Finnegans Wake is the richest, most indulgent, full-fat ice cream of a book and taking an entire semester-long class on any single text was already indulgent, so taking *Finnegans Wake* felt like an impractical and extravagant thing to do under the circumstances, which is why I did it. It felt like a fuck-you to someone. Not God, but someone.

The class on *Finnegans Wake* was one of the crown jewels of the college alongside Econ 101 and Justice, a low-level philosophy class that posed big questions about torture and altruism and the nature of evil, and that attracted hundreds of students during shopping period. Justice, *Finnegans Wake,* and Econ 101 were all held in the hallowed lecture hall behind Memorial Hall, with its tiered seating, dark wood, stained glass, and resounding echo that made everything the professor said sound like Morgan Freeman's voice of God.

Joyce and I had some history. The first time I tried reading *Finnegans Wake* was in high school. My tenth-grade English teacher, Ms. Lombardi, allowed me to come up with a syllabus for an informal independent study. I stacked the list with famously manic-depressive writers, bisexual modernists, etc. One of my most *inspired* Joycean essays ended up in the hands of the principal.

He called Ms. Lombardi into his office.

"Is she going to jump off a roof anytime soon? Should I be worried?"

Ms. Lombardi for her part said that the principal was just being sexist, classist, a xenophobe, and no friend of Joyce, but she did gently ask me if I was suicidal. I said that I was not.

For the spring semester, the Peabody reassigned me to the Vault, a building across the street where the museum kept its overflow and endeavored to forestall the inevitable transformation of ancient artifacts into dust. Five floors filled with racks and racks of tray after tray of artifacts from all over the world: tons of boxes of broken pottery, scraps of ceramic and terra-cotta. There were other artifacts in storage, too, objects it seemed sinful for me to even lay eyes on: a Peruvian funeral mask in the shape of a crocodile, a flute in the shape of a man holding a flute, his face painted black, white, and red, a khipu painted around his neck.

I was assigned to Isabella Gomes, a Brazilian conservator who looked exactly like Lily Tomlin. She was warm and chatty and prone to complaint, and as soon as she found out I was taking Portuguese, she began to terrorize me by speaking to me only in Portuguese and not responding unless I spoke Portuguese back to her. Isabella usually worked with ceramics. When I met her, she was working on a Spanish blue-and-white porcelain plate that was in pretty bad shape because the conservation techniques used in the '70s had damaged the plate more than time had.

Isabella was also in charge of making sure objects in the upcoming khipu exhibit were properly mounted and ready for display. Khipus had begun arriving from museums and private collections, encased in glass and protected by custom-made wooden crates. Some were of known provenance—discovered in colonial church cellars, highland villages, fort excavations, grave sites. Others were entirely unknown. Maybe pillaged by adventurers who kept the fibers as souvenirs or sold them off to wealthy collectors. The most valuable ones were colorful and complete, but the Peabody would also be showing smaller khipus, tangled khipus, and broken scraps, too, if only to underscore the rarity of the perfect ones.

"What's the connection between the khipu and the plates?" I asked.

"That's more in the curator's wheelhouse. I'm just here to restore this plate and you are here to help me."

My official job was to scan all the documents in the objects' provenance folders and then manually input the card information to be fully digitized. I usually did this on an old MacBook in a cramped, yellow-lit office, but some days Isabella asked me to follow her doing this or that.

"It would be super helpful if you could just carefully count these," Isabella said, gesturing to a cart full of cardboard boxes of terra-cotta shards, "and write the number in each box on one of these," she said, gesturing to a stack of Post-it notes, "and then move on to the next box. Start with these two and let's see how much we can get done today. All righty, off you go."

I put on my blue nitrile gloves and picked up a piece of terra-cotta the size of a box of cigarettes. *One. Two. Three. Thirty-six. Thirty-seven. Thirty-eight. Seventy-two. Seventy-three. FUCK.* I lost count many times, there were so many of them and they all looked the same.

None of the broken slabs of pottery mattered individually. We were counting them because we wanted to know how many we had; it was accounting, accounting again. I couldn't stop thinking about Roberto Bolaño's *2666,* which I had just finished reading.

There is a chapter called "The Part About the Crimes," part three, I believe. It's a police blotter–style account of the girls and women murdered in the fictional Santa Teresa, a stand-in for Ciudad Juárez.

Killing one woman is called femicide. Killing them en masse is called feminicide. Bolaño wrote about the deaths of these women and girls without consecrating the violence by turning it into art. He matter-of-factly listed the name of each woman or girl, their age, how their bodies were injured, and desecrated, and disposed of, and the person who found them. It was the little details that tore my heart, the women with underwear around their knees, white cotton undies with little bows on the side.

One. Two. Three. Twenty-four. Thirty-five. Thirty-nine. Eighty-one.

It was very hard to not blame my classmates. They were right here, playing Ultimate Frisbee and squash, buying pot from local Cambridge kids, fueling the crisis in Mexico. It wasn't a moralistic stance. It was horror at the horror. I was part of the same ecosystem as the girls in Juárez passed hand to hand. I was part of the same ecosystem as the boys thrown in Rikers if they so much as looked at a dime bag of marijuana. But I was also part of the same ecosystem as my classmates, that was part of the horror, too. Did my classmates ever think of us? I wanted to reach my hand into their brains through their ears and scratch in new grooves with my acrylic nails and then they would care, it was an untapped neural pathway, it just needed a little prodding along.

Counting the pieces also reminded me of the beloved rosary my grandmother gifted me for my First Communion: white, plastic, glow-in-the-dark. You're not supposed to wear a rosary around your neck but I did it. Anyway, that's what this job felt like, like a sin and a crime and an honor.

"Isabella, if there is an object from the upcoming exhibit I want to look at briefly, up close, but I wouldn't touch it, I would just look at it, who would I ask, hypothetically?"

"You can touch them, depending on what the object is, what it's made out of, what condition it's in," Isabella said, pointing to the box of disposable nitrile gloves with her chin. "I'd be happy to bring out anything for you. Just fill out a research request form, email it to me, and we'll go from there."

I wanted to touch a khipu. I had heard so much about them. It would be an honor to touch one even just through the film of a glove. It would definitely be a sin. I imagined it would feel brittle and dry, like damaged hair. Right in my hands—the end of an empire and the violent beginning of a new race, a race that was mine.

For the Inca people, visual input was not enough. They valued a multisensorial engagement with the world in ways we might never understand. There was something romantic in the fact that in order to properly read a khipu you needed to be able to differentiate—by touch—different kinds of Andean furs, woolens, and hair. Llama fibers did not feel the same as guanaco, alpaca, viscacha, and meaning could be encoded there. You needed to know those animals like the back of your hand. For this reason, Dr. Murphy called the khipu "the vernacular of small creatures." I found it funny that Dr. Murphy believed the vernacular of small creatures was to be found on their bodies. Maybe she thought their bodies were archives, too.

I played this game as a kid where I thought of a really gross or unfriendly looking animal, like a maggot or a possum, and tried to feel love for it, tried to find lovable things about the animal, and if I couldn't do it, then I told myself God was going to curse my family to racism and xenophobia for the rest of our lives because I had not heeded Christ's words in Matthew 25:40: *Truly I tell you, whatever you did for one of the least of these brothers and sisters of mine, you did for me.* The vernacular of small creatures is dreaming of vengeance. I remember every animal I've seen as roadkill, every single one.

I tossed and turned that night in bed after sending off my research request form. I played Don Omar's "Virtual Diva" loud into my headphones, alternating between imagining myself in his music video and planning my outfit for my private sitting with the khipu. The outfits melted into each other. They were the same outfit.

A camera from Byron had been waiting for me in the mailroom when I returned to campus, a little black handheld Panasonic camcorder with a screen that flipped out on the side.

There was an accompanying note on personalized stationery.

Catalina—

Am thinking we should experiment with an auto-ethnographic methodology. What does the world look like through Catalina's eyes? Your own view. Harvard. Family. Impending graduation. Film yourself doing what comes naturally, and send the footage over to me whenever.

BW

I believed Byron Wheeler's interest in the ethical representation of his subjects was sincere. I also saw how I could make quite the story.

Working with his dad brought Nathaniel and me closer. Nathaniel revered his father. In public, Byron Wheeler was known for being quick-tempered, prone to excess, a little reckless, a little messy—he could do a better job at hiding his infidelities, for example—but he was brilliant, which absolved him of everything. Nathaniel believed his father was a genius by any measure, an iconoclast with impeccable taste. Byron's creative interest in me seemed to validate Nathaniel's romantic interest in me so Nathaniel began treating me like a girlfriend, which is not something I had agreed to.

Byron Wheeler seems to have been so excited by the idea of this short that he brought it up at dinner with his family. His son, my Nathaniel, felt blindsided by the news of my status.

"Why didn't you tell me?" Nathaniel said as we walked to the Starbucks right off the Quad.

"I'm sorry."

"I'm just hurt that you didn't feel like you could trust me."

"I'm sorry, I'm sorry, I tried so many times but it never seemed like the right time."

"No, I'm sorry."

Nathaniel reached for my hand and interlaced his fingers in mine.

"You make me so mad."

"Mad in what way?"

"All the ways, Catalina."

Nathaniel and I began to meet in smaller and smaller places— like any empty stairwell at the Peabody during my lunch breaks— and we began to consider each other the most exciting people in the world, which is what meeting someone in increasingly smaller spaces will do. Everything that moved my flesh was typically in the minor tones, cumbias, boleros, the Hava Nagila, the Locrian mode in Björk. But I had not yet tried tenderness from a man who hadn't hurt me. I had not yet tried having my tears kissed away by a starry-eyed boy with beautiful hair. I had not yet tried E major in the spring. That I had not tried.

I got out of bed and found the video camera Byron Wheeler sent me. I pointed it at myself. In the dark, the highlights of my face were a radiant nightclub blue.

"This is a meditation on what being American means to me. If I could be any American living or dead, I'd choose to be Lauren London. When I saw her in Jay-Z and Pharrell's 'Frontin'' music video, I rewound the video over and over because she was so freaking pretty and I wanted to look like her. I'm not totally sure what lip gloss she's wearing in that video, but I believe it was either MAC Lipglass or a Lancôme Juicy Tube. She is also in Snoop Dogg's 'Drop It Like It's Hot' video, you know the tongue-popping? She popped her tongue in that one."

I pressed Stop, content with my camerawork and extemporaneous brilliance. I relaxed my face muscles, finally, unclenched my jaw, and went to sleep.

* ˙

Nathaniel belonged to a group of boys on campus known as the Bywater boys. Membership included him, Robert "Bobby" Dawley, and James "Just James" Arbuckle. They were well read, fluent in German, and itching for a shoot-out in section. They were known as the Bywater boys because they were disciples of enfant terrible historian of World War II, Sir Godfrey Bywater, a rumored close friend of Tony Blair. Their working group on Marx's *Capital* met once a week, on Wednesdays. Technically it was a graduate-level working group but exceptions were made for the Bywater boys. I knew Bobby and James through Nathaniel, and while we were not friends, we had begun to find ourselves in the same rooms and we nodded when we saw each other.

That's how I first heard they were throwing around the idea of starting a left-leaning literary magazine dedicated to anti-capitalist essays, stories, and poetry that examined social issues with the rigor of academia, but in a style infinitely more accessible than academia could ever be.

I dismissed the idea at first, but Nathaniel was serious and kept pressing for my approval.

One Friday, Nathaniel and I grabbed an early dinner at Adams House, the dorm closest to the train station, so that I could take the T to South Station to jump on the first available BoltBus to New York. I had to go home that weekend because my grandfather secured an audience with Luis Ruiz, known to everyone as Don Luis, a mediator, fixer, advocate, tax preparer, public notary, and occasional travel agent. It was the first time I saw my grandfather lift a finger to forestall his deportation, and I had to be there.

We were the first ones in the dining hall and everything we said boomed through the space.

"How would it be different from $n+1$?" I asked, setting my tray down.

"It would be nothing like $n+1$," Nathaniel said, "$n+1$ has become a parody of itself."

I had no idea what that meant but I had learned that accusing a cultural institution of being a parody of itself was always a legitimate opinion and usually a conversation-ender.

"Catalina, you could have a column! What was the column you proposed to *The Advo*?"

"It was called In Defense Of and I was going to defend maligned public figures, like Eliot Spitzer."

"Of all people. Let's circle back to that one."

"When is your first issue?"

"Aiming for September? Like a fall issue. The commihomies are going to push for earlier but I'm the one who's actually handling the logistics—"

"I hate that word."

"Which word?"

"*Commihomies*. It's an ugly word and it ought not be a word at all."

"I'll stop talking entirely if you want me to." His tone was playful but I didn't let it go.

"Isn't Robert starting some sketchy biotech company? That's a lot on his plate."

"It's not sketchy. Why does that matter? Because he's not a coal miner, he can't be a communist?"

"You know coal miner communists?"

"*Robert* intends for the company to be profitable within the first year and then it can serve as a corporate front for comrades in other countries."

"You're kidding me."

"That's what he says."

"This isn't a joke, Nathaniel."

"Nobody said it was!"

I got up to leave. I was fuming. But this was not a good time to alienate any of the Wheelers. They were being so nice to me. Fanny Brice would keep her cool. I lowered my chin, looked down at Nathaniel, and offered a semblance of a smile.

"Come here," he said, standing up. He reached for the purple scarf I had wrapped around my neck several times, and pulled me toward him.

"Stay," he said. "Don't go. You're always going."

My body offered no resistance.

Every culture has its bogeyman. In the Andes, it's a figure called the pishtaco. The pishtaco is a foreigner, an outsider, sometimes a white European or a North American or a light-skinned mestizo from the capital who steals fat from the bodies of Native

Americans and uses that grease to fuel their technologies—guns, military vehicles, railroads. Modern-day pishtacos might be Petrobras executives, or anthropologists. The story of the pishtaco established a new kind of racial technology: the Native American as a source of life-giving fire for the white foreigner.

Don Luis's office was a tiny travel agency in Queens, cluttered with photographs of Don Luis with everyone from Bill Clinton to Rudy Giuliani to Marc Anthony and Don Francisco. Don Luis had existed since the beginning of time. He'd certainly been living in Queens for as long. Just knowing he was alive made me feel a little safer in the world. I wasn't the only one. Don Luis had an FBI file. Allegedly. He had the personal phone number of the NYPD police commissioner and he did his best to broker a relationship between immigrants and police. If the cops picked up an immigrant for something stupid like jumping a turnstile, they weren't required by law to involve ICE, and if officers had that kind of discretion, it helped to build goodwill. But first they tapped his phone for a little while, allegedly.

In the '90s, drug traffickers lured desperate poor young women in Colombia to serve as drug mules. They paid them to swallow condoms packed tight with cocaine and defecate the cocaine pellets when they arrived in America. The drug traffickers on the American side counted the pellets; if they were short by even one, or if the women got sick and were unable to excrete the contraband, they were killed. Do you want to know exactly how they died? Of course you do. The drug traffickers cut the girls open like they were cutting slices into a day-old casserole—that amount of careful, that amount of respect. Then they dumped their bodies. A lot of girls ended up dead in Queens and family members in Colombia called Don Luis when girls in their families disappeared. Whenever the cops found dead Colombian girls, they, too, called Don Luis. People collected money in restaurants and nightclubs and churches, which is how, little by little, from New York City busboys and landscapers and nannies, Don Luis pooled enough money to send the girls back.

Sometimes the girls' bodies were unclaimed. Don Luis had a priest friend come give them last rites, and then he paid to have them cremated.

Don Luis handed me and my grandfather a pamphlet titled *Repatriación y Usted* and explained he was trying to start a new venture.

"The idea is that we know death is going to catch up with all of us immigrants here in Queens. You are going to die here, old and without much savings, if any. You either surprise your family and let them scramble to come up with plans through their grief, or you can prepare for it. It's like life insurance, except the small monthly payment goes toward covering all the funeral arrangements after you die, including repatriation to your country of origin, in this case Colombia, but we want to expand to Ecuador and Peru as well."

"What an amazing idea," my grandfather said. "Too bad Latinos don't buy insurance."

"Abuelo!" I scolded.

"It's true," Don Luis said. "You ask any immigrant, 'Do you want to die here? Do you want your body buried here, or do you want your body sent back home where people can mourn you?' people are going to say, 'Yes, yes, me, me,' but *you* try selling insurance to Colombians."

We all laughed.

"It should be preferable to letting this country have our corpses," my grandfather said defiantly. "I, for one, will be buried in Ecuador."

I was hurt and surprised to hear my grandfather say he wanted to be buried in Ecuador. I had no way of getting to Ecuador. I would have nowhere to lay flowers. Whatever family of his re-mained, whether or not they actually cared if he lived or died, they had a claim to his body and they had a claim to the mourning and grief. Interesting.

I had no desire to see Ecuador for myself. I'd heard enough. It didn't seem like the place for me. Still, sometimes I typed my aunt and uncle's address in Google Earth and looked at the street view. I fantasized about my grand return all the time. I would be famous and successful. I would be wearing a white pantsuit with a white bra underneath. If god—no, if a genie—told me I could have the bra of my dreams, I would say ribbons and bows, lots and lots of ribbons and bows. There is the question of how to keep an all-white outfit clean. In my dreams, I can walk in heels. I don't have flyaways and my slicked-back bun is *impeccable.* The part that stumps me is the earrings. I cannot stand having ear-rings on my ears. I mean, I *owned* earrings, if only just hoop ear-rings, from infant-size hoops to ones that almost grazed my shoulders. The small ones were real gold, the big ones were from Forever 21. I just never wore them. In my dreams, I can tolerate wearing hoops all day long so I wear hoops all day long.

I would go around local museums to see if I could spot any Conquest-era objects, I'm thinking dusty Bibles and old-timey guns, I would definitely get ceviche, and I would definitely eat everything. I do not believe I would get any foodborne or water-borne illnesses because I was born with a UTI and an *H. pylori* infection—my pediatrician says that is medically impossible but that's what the doctor who pulled me out of my mother had me hospitalized for. What I'm trying to say is I believe my body's constitution can handle a lot. I would want to see the Cotopaxi. I would not try to climb it. I just wanted to look up, memorize it, then jump back on the first flight back to LaGuardia. I had planned on going to see my aunt and uncle, now just my aunt. She would ask me how I was doing, and it would be very clear that I was doing incredible. I was doing fantastic, I was confident and capable and calm and collected, I had money and I was beautiful and also a genius. I had great legs. I spoke so many languages. I had a degree from every Ivy League school in the country, even Dartmouth. I had an infectious laugh. I tossed my head back when I laughed, like Julia Roberts on *Letterman*. Children loved me. The entire extended family would love me. I would make an impression. I would imprint onto them and they would be sad for the rest of their days, sending me away was the worst mistake of their lives. They really missed out. They were going to think about me forever.

Don Luis put on his reading glasses and extended his hand.

"Let's get to your letter," he said.

Don Luis read under his breath, producing from his throat a sharp whistle.

"Look, Francisco," he said sternly, "I can't sugarcoat it for you, this is a pretty direct order of deportation. But you can fight, if you want to fight it, if you have it in you."

"We are fighting!" I interjected. "We have a lawyer. He just filed a motion to reopen the proceedings!"

"That's good, mija," Don Luis continued. "It does buy you some time. Sometimes the courts move slow. With that filed, any ICE officer can't just disappear him overnight, but at the end of the day, I need to say, our odds aren't great."

My grandfather slouched in his chair and sucked his teeth.

"Mierda."

"On the other hand, you have a child in college, at Harvard, she graduates in June. If you want to try fighting it, we can go to the press and say, 'Look, I want to see my granddaughter graduate college, I've raised her since she was small, her parents are dead, and she is so close.' Who knows? Maybe if there's public outcry, there could be a miracle."

I sat up taller.

"That's why I'm making a documentary film this semester at school. It might help, right?"

My grandfather let out a brief rumbling growl and turned away.

I never got the sense that my grandfather lived his life on my timeline. Quite the opposite. When I graduated high school, my grandmother confessed to me that he had tried to send me back to Ecuador when I was sixteen because he didn't like what America was "doing" to me. She talked him out of it. I had no idea they were making these negotiations about my life in a back room. My grandfather took a long swig from a bottle of cranberry juice. It wasn't spiked. He just liked cranberry juice. Sitting there was easier for me if I pretended I was an up-and-coming writer on assignment in Jackson Heights, profiling these charismatic men. Only a writer could transfigure their stories into literature. Once they were literature, they could no longer be disappeared.

Don Luis began addressing me.

"It might help. It might not help. They'll deport anyone now."

At home, my grandmother was uncharacteristically stormy. She sat in front of the TV with a sewing kit and a stack of clothes to bring in and hem. She kept pricking herself and saying, Carajo! I took out my computer and I was surprised to see Abél Morrison's name on the mass email Nathaniel sent out announcing *Disrupt,* a Web magazine for big ideas, inaugural issue forthcoming. Abél was listed as a contributing editor. I was listed as a founding member but I had nothing to do with that. Kyle, for example, was also dragged into this and his only contribution thus far had been the logo. Oh god we were founding members, weren't we? I emailed Abél immediately.

To: Abél Morrison
From: Catalina Ituralde
Subject: !!
3:18 P.M.

Abél Morrison, do you find yourself in a delicate situation and perhaps in need of help? Are you being blackmailed, for example, or extorted?!!! Because I saw you listed as a contributing editor!!!!! for that crazy magazine.

To: Catalina Ituralde
From: Abél Morrison
Subject: Re: !!
8:45 P.M.

Jajaja I think it's good they're seeking advice! You might be surprised to know catalina that this is not my first time working with obnoxious college radicals. It's how you build support!

Abrazos.

That night, for my next video for Byron, I narrated an entirely fabricated story about how my grandparents met.

When my grandfather met my grandmother, he knew he had to marry her, but her father wouldn't allow it, so he marched into town on his horse and he picked her up and stole her away. She sat on the horse like a man. My grand-

mother was the town beauty. She had dark curly hair and a
melancholic air, which my grandfather found irresistible.

I went to the kitchen to play my grandmother the clip. She was
washing the dishes and turned off the faucet to watch.

"Catalina! None of this is true!"

"Can you prove it?"

"Prove what?"

"Can you prove with irrefutable documentary evidence that
this did not happen?"

"Noooo, stupid."

"Why not?"

"How could a piece of paper prove I wasn't stolen away on a
horse like a sack of rice? You're so stupid!"

"So it's true?"

She laughed. "You are so, so stupid."

I smiled at her, then felt guilty for having fun with my grandmother while my grandfather was suffering. I felt so bad for him,
asleep on the couch. I woke him up gently and told him if he
didn't get to bed he'd wake up with back pain. He kissed my forehead and waddled to his bedroom.

"I'm going to go make more videos," I said to my grandma.
"Don't make noise."

The camera was addictive. I liked the heft of it, the suggestion
of a living thing in my hand. I recorded myself lip-syncing to Amy
Winehouse and played the footage back to myself. I hated my
face, I hated my voice, I hated my body, I hated myself for feeling
a flutter at my own likeness, attributing to Nathaniel, like a cow-
ard, the desire I so patently felt toward myself.

I uploaded the videos to Dropbox for Byron and then sent a
link to Delphine. I really wanted her to watch them for some
reason. I even texted her to alert her to my email containing the

Dropbox link. And then I waited. For hours. I was nervous. Clearly I had done something wrong but I did not know what that was. I just knew it was bad. I knew it revealed the nasty truth about myself, which is that I was vain and selfish and also a liar. Finally, around 11:00 P.M., I texted her.

Did you get my email?

Yeah, I did. I thought it was good

You sound mad?

I thought it was good! I'm a little concerned it comes across as stereotypical.

Stereotypical how? The part about the horse?

I'm not sure this is the best use of your talents, hon.

I was gutted but I swallowed it quickly.

Delphine, it turned out, was not enthusiastic about my work with Byron.

"Catalina, you can't be serious," she'd said when I told her about the project. "You know why he is doing this, don't you?"

I knew, I knew.

Around the time of the Oscar nomination, an open letter addressed to Byron circulated on the Internet. *Wheeler's fondness for South America strives to be apolitical and in doing so he rejects the current-day realities of the subjects in the countries he presents to Western audiences. Wheeler also aestheticizes and romanticizes Latin America without showing any awareness of geopolitical realities.* Delphine suspected this had something to do with his sudden interest in the undocumented but she told me to follow my heart.

Delphine, sunshine, angel, CrossFit, made it her personal mission to make me complete my thesis. I was her project. We met twice a week for work sessions in the library café, computers side by side for accountability, phones zipped up in backpacks under the table. I hated her for it, but sometimes it helped. I had decided to write about the feminicide chapter in Roberto Bolaño's *2666*. I didn't know if it would stick, but at least I'd be able to hand Sandoval some pages. We were in the midst of one such miserable session when I spotted Nathaniel walking toward us.

"Hey, I was thinking, let's go skiing this weekend," he said.

I glanced at Delphine. She didn't look up.

"Where is there skiing in Boston?"

"No, silly. Vermont. I'll book a hotel. I'll drive. It'll be so fun."

Nathaniel had not acknowledged Delphine and Delphine had not acknowledged Nathaniel and I did not know if this was common among strangers, or if I was meant to introduce them to each other, and if so, would introducing Nathaniel to Delphine give Nathaniel the impression I was serious about him? I just sat there in silence burrowing even deeper in the discomfort.

"I don't know how to ski," I protested.

"I'll teach you." He leaned in to kiss me on the cheek, adjusted his backpack, and was gone.

Would it be so bad to give him a real chance? I had never let myself feel soft in a boy's hands, lowered myself into the fantasy of being a girl for a boy, the water is freezing at first but then it gets warm, just really nice and sunny, a perfect day at the pool. So Nathaniel and I are fit, healthy, thriving young professionals, we have our own lives, we don't see each other every day, but we are in a committed and monogamous relationship. We try to have dinner together as often as we can, he comes by my place after work on Thursdays, usually, which is when his workdays are the longest, and I have a watercress salad prepared with my home-made salad dressing, we don't eat much, I've lost my appetite recently, he comes over late and he fucks me everywhere but my bed; caught up in the moment, against the kitchen sink, I tell him to come inside me. I tell him I'll just take emergency contraception in the morning, and in the dark, Nathaniel whispers, *Maybe we can keep it.*

It is the stupidest idea in the world. I do not want to have a baby. But I do want to have *his* baby, him specifically. I like Na-thaniel, and I like what liking Nathaniel says about me. I want him to choose me, and he does. He brings warmed bottles of milk to me in the middle of the night. For the baby. I don't know if Nathaniel understands what I am offering him, which is the li-cense to kill me. When the nurse hands me our baby, Nathaniel stands over us and looks at us so lovingly. Importantly he does not look at the baby first. He kisses the baby's head but doesn't take his eyes off me. I look down at our baby, exhausted, a halo above my messy bun. I'd made life.

We have sleepless nights. We have help, we are so fortunate to have help, but I want to do it myself, I am really hands-on, I'm a really hands-on mom, and Nathaniel is a really hands-on dad, but we are both still young and we're just two kids trying to do this thing called life, some days we survive off just cereal, and some-times my grandmother comes over and takes the baby for a walk so I can do some basic chores and the entire time I'm supposed to be doing the laundry, or putting away the dishes, I'm giving Nathaniel a blow job in the shower. When I breastfeed the baby, Nathaniel lies on the foot of the bed reading Joyce on his back, and then he turns to me, looks at me lewdly, following the veins on my milk-engorged breast, the irritated nipple in and out of the baby's mouth. He puts the book down and crawls to me. I put the creature aside.

When he walks home from the school bus, I am happy to see my rosy-cheeked child and note how much he looks like his father. I married a good man. His parents think he married a really good girl. That's what they say. *Our son married a great girl.* We rarely go to friends' weddings but when we do, we stop at a five-star hotel and we do everything short of heroin. Well, not him. Nathaniel abstains. He likes seeing me like this, increasingly uninhibited. I say something pitiful and he asks me to clarify, knowing full well that I never know what I mean, on the chance I might reveal something about myself I would hold on to tighter if I was sober. Nothing you do in a hotel room ever counts. Nathaniel always says he has no unexplored desires or fantasies and I say, Look, it's dark, the door is closed, nobody's here, nobody has to know. He looks at me tenderly, the way he used to look at me when we were college sweethearts and he said he liked when I wore my yellow dress. We shower in the morning. We look clean, we smell like expensive soap and perfume, we are wearing coordinating linens and tasteful gold jewelry. High-end but quiet. He kisses me on the cheek as I brush my teeth and he hugs me from behind. I rest my weight against his chest, lean my head back to get a look of that handsome face and sink my cuticle scissors into the approximate whereabouts of his spleen.

"First you're doing a trauma porn movie with the dad, something you said you'd never do, and now you're *skiing* with the son? *Skiing?* Skiing doesn't really sound like you. Are you sure you're not trying to change just so this white boy will like you?"

I could not really hear Delphine because I was still daydreaming. So far I had been to the following states: Massachusetts, New Jersey, Connecticut, New York, and Pennsylvania. Now I was

going to Vermont. I was excited, but I did not confess this to Delphine and I would never, ever tell Nathaniel. But I did tell my
grandma.

"Are you going to Aspen?" my grandma asked.

"No, Vermont."

"Oh, why not Aspen?"

"What do you mean why not? Because we're going to Vermont."

"Mariah Carey goes to Aspen every year. There's a video of her
coming out of a restaurant in Aspen wearing a tiny black coat
cropped at the waist, fur collar—probably real fur, you know how
I feel about that. But the point is she was wearing stilettos! Her
bodyguards had to each grab an arm and help her walk! Who
walks in the snow in stilettos?"

"Mariah."

"Did you know she's Hispanic? Her dad is a Black Venezuelan.
Good for her." Her voice became softer. "You don't have a good
coat."

"The one I have is fine."

"No, Catalina, it is not. You look homeless. I'm going to deposit
some money into your bank account so you have a little extra for
whatever comes up."

"Aw, thank you, Abuela."

"Just remember to bring me a souvenir," she said excitedly.
"Like a magnet."

The drive through Vermont was very scenic. The evergreen
trees were thick with virgin snow and the sky was milky white. It
looked as cold as it was. What can I say about New England after
a snowfall that hasn't been said before and better by Dickinson
and Frost? I looked over at Nathaniel and felt the color rising to
my cheeks. He was beautiful.

"What do your friends say about me?" I asked.

"What do you mean? Why?"

I shrugged.

"I'm curious."

"'Spanish girls are small and very sexual,' you know, the Carmen Miranda bullshit, Orientalism," he joked.

"Ah, yes," I said. "Edward Said."

We stopped by a gas station for gas and snacks. I got lost in thought for a second. I had never gone skiing, had zero idea what it entailed, and I didn't know how much money my grandma had put in my bank account. I'd have to pace myself.

"Hey," Nathaniel said, and softly touched my back. He was holding a large Evian water and some Chex Mix. I smiled up at him, and took a blue Gatorade out of the fridge. When we went up to pay, Nathaniel said, "I got it," and his wallet was already out. There was no time to bicker. He asked for a pack of condoms, without saying anything to me, which made me feel embarrassed and adult. The smoothness and rudeness of the gesture by a highway at three in the afternoon was impressive. The guy behind the register was Mexican. I averted eye contact with both men.

Nathaniel and I arrived at our cabin at four in the afternoon. We barely managed to put our stuff inside and close the door before we started kissing. "Don't say anything, don't say anything," he whispered to me, pulling away at everything. We fell to the floor. I climbed on top of him, and from this perch I saw his face, a face from an old Tommy Hilfiger ad. I was afraid Nathaniel was going to tell me he loved me when he came. I would be so embarrassed if he did and I held his face in my hands the whole time, hoping that he would. His dark brown curls in between my fingers felt like owning an American Girl doll I could give to a less fortunate girl after I was done. I kissed him with deep concentration, hoping he knew what a good man I thought he was, wondering if he would choke me if I asked. I had wanted him for so long.

He was the Roman wing at the Met, and I wanted to carve into him with a knife.

The moon was out in full drag, the fucking moon, loud as hell, forcing moonlight onto my face. Nathaniel fumbled for a condom while I waited with my eyes closed. I used my hands to feel for the part of his face I liked to think about sometimes, which will seem masculine if I say jaw and feminine if I say cheekbones, but in his face they were both. I didn't want the animal parts of this. The movie, that was sex, too.

He fell asleep on top of me. I was too young to have men falling asleep on top of me. Everything felt painfully reflective. Sometimes I thought about how many men had masturbated thinking of me throughout my life and I hoped the number was really high, that I hit every demographic, that it was dirty and hot and taboo, but I did not like to think about individual men doing it, dumb men, ugly men, men without talent, men whose talents I found boring or superfluous, men who thought they were a big fuckin' hoot, men who were in any way effortful. I did not want to think about how young I was when I entered their minds in this way, if it was on a day when I was sad, if they had been presented to me as safe men, entrusted to guide me when I came to them littler and powerless, like a professor or the cabdriver who took me to the bus station at 3:00 A.M. while I slept in the back seat. I tried not to think about it. But I did I did I did.

There was a Denny's across the parking lot. I quickly got dressed, I threw on my pale yellow dress and grabbed Nathaniel's parka. He was sound asleep. I kissed him on the forehead, then snuck out and crossed the lot to the Denny's, desperate to do something I could not take back. I sat next to some guy in a booth, not across from him. He looked lonely. Lonely people are up for anything. I ordered a coffee and pancakes, then leaned back against the seat so that our arms were touching. I saw that he liked it. I then relaxed my body so that his right arm brushed across my left breast and I simply did not wince, I knew that to light the fuse all I had to do was not stop him. He made his way under my dress and then inside the underwear that Nathaniel had called lingerie not long before, waiting a few seconds before pressing his fingers inside me. I stared at the screen of my Black-Berry, careful not to make any noise.

＊ •

"What is night skiing?" I asked when I got out of the shower and found Nathaniel dressed in his ski clothes, twirling in his socks out of excitement.

"It's really fun, you'll love it. Maybe dry your hair, though. It's freezing out and your hair will turn to ice."

"Oh, okay, I'll blow-dry my hair. I definitely want to go with you but I'll just watch, if that's okay."

"Whyyyy? You don't want to go?"

I shook my head and scrunched up my nose. I had told Nathaniel I would go skiing with him, but I didn't say I was going to try to *learn* to ski. Going skiing refers to the entire *experience,* the snow, the lodge, the Top 40 hits coming from speakers I couldn't see, the outfit. No? He didn't buy it, either. I had zero desire to ski. Skiing involved playing with the odds, however slight, that I was going to have a bad fall and break my neck or spine and become paralyzed. Becoming paralyzed, stuck in my body with my intact brain, under the care of my grandparents, was the most horrifying scenario I could imagine.

"Come on. Don't be a bad sport. At least try."

"I know I'm going to be really bad at it, and I don't like doing things I know I'm going to be bad at."

"Please? For me?"

"No," I said, surprised by the implication.

"Do you feel like you're too cool to ski, is that it?"

I thought about it.

"Kind of," I said reluctantly.

"Okay," he said, walking away. I was stunned. I had been joking, kind of! I stomped off in the opposite direction, in the direction of the lodge. I was relieved to find a mostly empty restaurant on the top floor. I grabbed a corner table and ordered cheesecake and a martini, the right-seeming food and drink for after a fight in a cabin. I only had my phone, iPod, and wallet on me, and my phone wasn't working at all. It had lost signal miles and miles ago. Praying it was charged, I took out my iPod and toggled to the original cast recording of *Rent*.

A family sat down at the table next to mine, despite the entire floor being empty, and made a big show of domestic bliss. The child, a toddler in a pink princess dress and oily blond hair, looked happy. I thought: *Why her? What about this child makes white Americans salivate at even the hypothetical scenario of having to use a gun to protect her? Where is the war that was being waged illegally on my behalf?* The child's parents did the things people do, send food back, talk over the server, interrupt each other, burp. They were nothing special. That was the most humiliating part of all of this. The rest of the world is plundered and bombed so rich white people can eat Caesar salad with each other and be inane.

We set off to Boston early the next morning, before breakfast was served out in the lodge, disque to avoid traffic. We'd never spent this many hours together and I noticed Nathaniel's irritation when I asked too many questions about his encounters with various animals. No, he had not seen bison. Yes, he had seen many, many deer. Of course he'd seen bears. Who *hasn't* seen a raccoon? He'd seen glimpses of groundhogs, sure. It's not like they hung around. About an hour into the drive, we stopped for gas and Nathaniel ducked into a small grocery store for snacks. We were starving. I waited in the car. I felt cozy riding shotgun. I've always loved a good long drive. Nathaniel returned with two cheeseburgers wrapped in foil and a coffee for him and a strawberry milkshake for me. I felt swarmed by butterflies.

"Craziest fucking thing," he began, pulling out of the parking lot. "I was in the line to check out and it was taking forever and I see that the person holding up the line is a lady paying for her groceries with food stamps, which—good for her—and I look at what the cashier is ringing up and it is *various,* as in more than one, seriously expensive cuts of steak."

"Are you fucking serious?" I said slowly, sounding out every word.

Nathaniel glanced at me quickly, searching my face for clues on how to read my tone.

"Are you okay being this much of a cliché?" I continued.

"I don't know where this is coming from," he said carefully, his eyes glued to the icy road.

"My family was on food stamps. Did you know that?"

This was not true. No one in my family qualified for food stamps because of our legal status.

"I'm sorry I said something hurtful, and I'm so, so happy your family was able to benefit from food stamps, but I'm talking about something else entirely. We're not talking milk and eggs here."

"It's not called food stamps, by the way, *asshole,*" I said, now through hot, angry tears. "It's called EBT."

"Okay, EBT, baby, this is ridiculous. Let's stop fighting." It was his first time calling me baby.

"Fuck off, Nathaniel."

"I don't appreciate you cursing at me."

"I don't appreciate anything about you right now."

"Hey, hey, hey, Catalina, breathe," he said. "Calm down, just breathe."

When has that ever worked?

The way you throw yourself out of a moving car is, you wait until you're under 35 mph, you imagine you're a frog, protect your head, and jump and roll. You're obviously going to get hurt. That's part of the fun. Before going into a car with a man, I look at the child lock toggle hidden on the side of the door, and I flick it off. I am never inside a locked car with a man. My body was covered in layers of clothing—tights under my jeans, a fuzzy sweater under my coat, gloves—but my face was exposed, and the gravel scratched its way across my chin, my cheeks, my nose, as I rolled to the side of the road. My face! My beautiful face!

Nathaniel stopped the car and ran over. "What the fuck!" he yelled. "What the fuck!"

"I'm okay," I said, standing up quickly to prove just how okay I was. I was dizzy. "Just take me home."

"The fuck, Catalina, there's blood all over your face. I should take you to the hospital."

"I didn't break anything. Please just take me home." I spoke in a puppy-mill-puppy quiver. He couldn't say no.

We drove the remainder of the way in silence.

✳

At the Peabody the next morning, Isabella Gomes had a khipu laid out on the table for me. It was a funerary khipu on loan from a private collector. This one had clearly arrived to us through the efforts of a grave robber. It was found tied around the waist of a deceased highlander in Peru. A lot of khipus were found in mausoleums. The Spanish hadn't looked there, but the archaeologists did. The khipu looked so small and thirsty, so deserving of a sit under a shady tree.

I hesitated.

"It's okay, you can get closer, you can even touch it if you put on these gloves." She motioned to the box.

It felt wrong.

*   *

I had been ignoring her emails for weeks, and I stood her up the last time we were supposed to meet, so when Professor Sandoval sent me a matter-of-fact email inviting me to coffee at Finale sometime that week, threatening that if I didn't show up she'd come up to my dorm and drag me there herself, I went.

"Here," Professor Sandoval began, pushing a ziplock plastic bag filled with tea bags across the table. "This is lino, in English it's called linden flower. I drink it every day. It's like chamomile, helps with stress."

"Thanks," I said, embarrassed and surprised by how early in the conversation I wanted to cry. I could tell she was trying to withhold a remark about the scratches on my face.

The server approached our table.

"I'll just have a cappuccino, thank you," said Professor Sandoval.

"Can I have a hot chocolate, please? That's it for me, thanks."

"Let's get something to share, how about that? The carrot cake looks good, or the Chocolate Symphony, that sounds fun. Maybe too much chocolate. We'll have a carrot cake? Yes? Yes, the carrot cake, thank you." She smiled warmly at the server.

I suspected Delphine got in touch with Professor Sandoval and told her something, maybe that she was worried about me, maybe something about my grandfather, and by default she was the professor closest to me as my advisor. I felt a lot of guilt over disappointing Sandoval. Harvard had not been admitting undocumented students for very long and each of us was like a guinea pig for them. So much was riding on me to do well here.

I took out a paper from a metallic pink folder in my tote bag. It was stapled at the left-hand corner, and lightly perfumed.

"Is this your literature review?"

We both knew that it was not.

"It's new. It's a little writing on the feminicides chapter in 2666."

"I don't know where to begin," she said evenly, eyes alternating between staring at her cake and my essay. Then she took out a pen and planner from her purse, wrote something on a piece of paper, tore it out, and passed it to me across the table.

Dolores Araya

"Who is Dolores Araya?"

"She's my therapist."

"Okay . . ."

"She's Chilean, and she isn't covered by Harvard insurance, but if you go see her, I'm sure she'll agree to an arrangement of some kind. I really like her. She works with the children of the disappeared."

"I don't know what to say."

"Promise me you'll look her up."

"I promise," I said.

We both knew that I would not.

When Professor Sandoval told me I needed therapy, I felt embarrassed because it was a teacher telling me that I had done something wrong. That is how I interpreted it. I hadn't kept my side of the street clean and I was drawing attention to myself. The therapist was going to just say this was about my dead parents and my dead uncle, maybe my aunt who was still alive in Ecuador doing this and that without me, eating salad and going for haircuts and knitting in front of the news. I was too cute and smart and interesting to have been damaged by such low-hanging fruit, could you imagine?

* ·

Byron had not exactly been blown away by the footage I sent him of my thoughts on Mariah Carey, my favorite North American mammals, and my grandparents' love story, but he emailed to say *some good stuff here!* and I sensed that he found some of it amusing. I also emailed him a link to a Pinterest board I had titled "My Mind." It included pictures of everything that inspired me: the Northern Lights, Bruce Springsteen's jeans, Kate Moss coming out of nightclubs, Diego Luna in *Y Tu Mamá También,* girls with bangs, parking lot birds, latte art. Byron confirmed receipt.

Preproduction came and went and before I knew it, it was March 4, the day of Byron's visit and also the coldest and windiest March 4 in twenty years. Harvard did not allow film or TV to shoot on campus but Byron hoped we could get away with it by pointing out he would not be using shots of the exterior, and the inside of my dorm room looked like the inside of any generic college dorm room.

I went to bed at 4:00 A.M. the night before partly because I was deep-cleaning my room and partly because I couldn't fall asleep. I woke up with a migraine and a sore neck. I mindlessly stepped out of bed and onto my headphones, breaking them. My headphones were Beats. My grandfather bought them off one of his friends, a hypebeast twenty-seven-year-old Mexican construction worker who didn't like them. That I liked rock and roll was one of the few and foundational facts that my grandfather knew about me and it made him proud, he told everyone I liked rock and roll, this is what he called it, he called it rocanrol. When I broke them, I felt a wave of vertigo and deep shame, as if I'd used a slur against my grandfather, reported him to ICE myself. I threw up, brushed my teeth, and threw up again, and brushed my teeth again. Then I skipped downstairs to let Byron and his cameraman in.

"Hey, you look nice," Byron said, schlepping tote bags of camera equipment. He introduced me to Ryan, his cameraman.

I looked at my reflection as the three of us passed by the mirror in the lobby. I wore black skinny jeans with a black leotard underneath. I pulled my hair back with a black ribbon and applied concealer over the still visible scrapes on my face. Did I really not look as sick as I felt?

I let them into my room.

"This is it," I said, arms open.

My dorm was a hundred-and-fifty-square-foot single with a twin-size bed against one wall, a tiny wooden desk against the opposite wall, and a bookcase in between. My bed was made nicely with a daisy-print comforter with matching sheets and pillowcases.

Ryan arranged a stack of packing boxes on the floor and began straightening out the books on my bookcase.

"Hey, while you guys are setting up, do I have time to run to the bathroom real quick?"

"Of course. Do what you need to do."

The bathroom was down the hall and I was lucky to find it empty. I brought down my shower caddy where I had preemptively stashed a bottle of cranberry juice with vodka ahead of Byron's visit. I took one, two, three good large gulps, gagged and dry-heaved horrendously, rinsed my mouth with mouthwash, and reapplied lip gloss.

Back in the room, the two were still settling in, screwing in lights and testing microphones.

I stiffly took my position at my desk, where Ryan had placed an open notebook and pen. Props. I was so aware of the camera.

"We'll start filming now, Catalina," Byron said. "I'll ask you some questions to get us started, to ease us in, while we mess around with specs and try to get you just right."

I had imagined that when the camera was on me, I would instinctively know how to move my body, Naomi Campbell doing some acting work in her spare time. But this was not to be. I became so self-conscious about the expressions I was making or not making that I forgot entirely how faces worked. I had to manually bring forth the thoughts that moved my face and body. I had to make myself blink.

"Catalina is such a pretty name. Where does it come from?"

"It's from a song called 'La Catalina.'"

"Ecuadorian?"

"I'm surprised you don't know it."

"Is it famous?"

"I don't know. You just seem to know everything I know."

"I'm going to throw some questions at you. You can say skip if you want, or we can come back to something later."

I nodded.

"Do you feel American?"

I was distracted by the camera operator. Ryan. Ryan, my man! Ryan was in his seventies. He looked nice. I tried to guess how much money he made. I wondered whether his parents were dead, and if they were still alive, I wondered what their secret was. Was it drinking beer and making love? That's what the oldest person in the world always says when they are interviewed once a year around New Year's. I wondered if Ryan had ever met RuPaul.

"Catalina? You there?"

"I was born in South America, now I live in North America, it would be hard to not feel American, so, yes, I do, because by definition I am."

I usually did not notice my body unless it was injured or being admired. *Be careful, you need to be more careful with your body,* my grandmother scolded, but *be careful* isn't actionable. I moved through physical space like a remote-control car controlled by a toddler. I sometimes forgot what it meant to have a body. But I did not for a second forget the camera was there.

"Can you stand by the window? Let's have you by the window. Do you have a backpack? Can you grab your backpack? Put a couple of books in it so it doesn't look flat. Okay, wear your backpack, use both straps. Stand at the window, looking outside, but turn around as if you're talking to a friend. Can you put your hand on the window? Here, let me show you."

He walked over and grabbed my hand, shook my arm up and down up and down, and said, "Relax, relax this arm." I closed my eyes and relaxed my arm, letting him coax my fingers out of a fist.

"Let's try some packing."

As per Byron's first point of inspiration, today I would be pretending to pack my room. The floor was hard and cold so I laid out a pink yoga mat I bought my freshman year in anticipation of all the yoga I planned on doing. I sat down cross-legged.

Most of my belongings were novels. Before Harvard I had never had a bookcase in my room. The past four years had been a blessing. I had my own bed, my own bookcase, my own door with two locks. But I did not tell him that. I put my shoulders back and concentrated on making my stomach look as flat as possible.

The first book that I brought down was *The Autobiography of Alice B. Toklas*. The second was *The Lion, the Witch, and the Wardrobe*. The third was *Open Veins of Latin America*. This was not on purpose. The only reason I had that book in the first place is because Nathaniel said it was his favorite book and he gave it to me.

"Wait, is that *Venas Abiertas*?"

"Yes, this copy is in English, though."

"I fucking love that book. Okay, put it back and then take it down again. Let's just do that a few times."

I had no doubt in my mind that Byron Wheeler loved this book, and I was eager to hear his meet-cute story about how he fell in love with Latin America.

As directed, I put the book back on the shelf, and then I put it back into the box, then back on the shelf, like those toy kittens that come out when you put a quarter in the little box.

The truth is, I've never read *Open Veins of Latin America*. There's something about Hugo Chávez's blurb on the cover that put me off. My grandfather did not love Hugo Chávez, but he often played me videos of his speeches from Venezuelan balconies to teach me oratory, a lost art in his opinion. It was a dictator's cadence, and my grandfather could do it perfectly. Anyway, another thing that kept me from reading the book is that Nathaniel told me to read it and I do not like it when boys tell me what to read.

Finally, my arms fell limp to my sides. I let the book fall. I was kneeling on my yoga mat, I wasn't shaking or anything, but something was wrong.

"Catalina?"

I felt trapped in my body. I couldn't move. I couldn't cry. I couldn't talk. Byron approached me.

"Hey," he said, his hand on my shoulder. "Are you okay?"

My face scrunched up to cry but I caught it and took deep breaths to try to steady myself.

"Okay, it's okay," I said. Over and over I said, "It's okay."

"Okay," he said, relieved. "Can we keep filming?"

I didn't answer. The camera kept rolling as Byron fussed around with the lighting. He clipped transparent-blue sheets on to the light fixtures. I started to cry like a baby pig.

Tell us what you love most about your grandfather.

What are your memories of Ecuador?

Catalina, what's the hardest thing about being a Dreamer?

Who's your favorite Beatle?

"George [hiccup] Harrison," I whimpered. I did not want to die without answering.

And it was like this for a while. I don't know whether it was five minutes or fifty. I was rescued by one of the dining hall workers. Martha was Irish and from Jamaica Plain. I suspected she was a Republican. Martha had bright red hair that always looked freshly dyed, she wore a small diamond crucifix around her neck, and she showed me pictures of her grandkids, and by grandkids she meant all the stray dogs and cats her incorrigible niece would not stop finding on the street and in kill shelters and bringing home to Martha.

"Mind you, I don't have a king-size mattress, okay? I have three dogs, all of whom want to sleep in my bed, of course, and seven cats. Seven cats! I tell my niece, 'You're crazy! You're crazy!' But I love her and I'm a softie, too, so, you know, I look the other way."

Usually, Martha sat at the entrance to my dormitory's dining hall where she swiped our IDs, so I saw her almost every morning and early evening. She had a front-row seat to my emotional state, more than most people, and I knew she liked me because when she saw me slouched in front of my laptop in the dining hall at 5:30 A.M. for the second time in a row, she had just come in, the kitchen wasn't even open yet, but she made me a coffee with cream and sugar and walked it over to me, shaking her head, looking genuinely mad. "Two nights in a row? You're going to do this two nights in a row?"

People in my dorm had the habit of taking food up to their rooms and then leaving the plates, mugs, and cutlery in the hallway as if they were in a hotel. As if we were in a hotel. We would eventually take the dinnerware back, plate by plate, mug by mug, but sometimes Martha would overhear the kitchen staff complain about a mysterious shortage of silverware, and she would lose her patience and do it herself. That day, Martha was making the rounds, pushing around a black cart, picking up our mess.

Martha paused by my open door and quickly took in the scene.

"Excuse me," she said firmly to Byron Wheeler. "Do you have a Harvard ID?"

"No, she let us in, we're friends of Catalina's, I'm a filmmaker—"

"Okay. If you don't have a Harvard ID, you can't be here."

"She let us in."

"Okay, but do you have a Harvard ID?"

"No, I'm not a student. I'm an alumnus. Look, I'm trying to help her."

"It's a yes or no question, sir. *Do you have a Harvard ID?* If you don't, you can't be here."

Byron looked aghast, but he didn't have a Harvard ID, and I did, and I no longer wanted him there. I watched as she escorted them out.

✳ •

It rained every single day in March. Maybe the sun came up and the sun went down but it had no impact on the appearance of the sky, which was sooty and gray around the clock. I felt quiet but my body was agitated and on the days that it rained torrentially, I went outside and put my face to the sky inviting the rain to rough me up. I didn't have it in me to talk to anybody at all. I retreated to the museum. In the Vault I could busy myself for hours with objects that also did not care to speak.

Josh emailed to say that with the motion to reopen now filed, we could expect to hear the immigration judge's decision by May. I didn't want to get my hopes up or anything, but I was fully anticipating a miracle. Miracles happened to me all the time. I prayed to God to express gratitude for all my privileges and blessings and to, by the way, ask for a huge fucking favor. I offered God so many things. I offered to give up chocolate, I offered to give up bread, I offered to dress more modestly and be less vain, more interested in His glory and not my own. I offered God my first-born. I offered God my own life in the form of Christian martyrdom. I could chop off my hair, slice off my breasts, deny sex to every man, refuse marriage to the king. Still, I knew there was a real chance my grandfather would not be there for my graduation, so I invited my grandparents to the opening of *The Khipu and Its Infinite Possibilities*. If he missed my graduation, he'd see none of the pomp and circumstance of the Harvard commencement, a celebration that spanned multiple days and involved men with top hats, regalia galore, uniformed men on horseback, Secret Service details, parrots, and taking in these sights, the totality of them, might have made all his years in this country worth it. The khipu exhibit opening wasn't that, but it was the only Harvard spectacle I could offer him. There would be speeches and wine.

On the Friday before spring break, my grandparents took the Chinatown bus from New York. My grandmother looked divine in a long, formfitting houndstooth dress, vintage pearls, a glittery silver clutch, and flip-flops. She carried her favorite pair of shoes, high-heeled Mary Janes with thick silver buckles, in her purse.

My grandfather just looked like my grandfather. He wore a pressed and crisp Harvard T-shirt tucked into colorfast Wrangler jeans. He shaved and combed his still very thick, partially gray hair backward into a wavy swoop.

My grandparents loved coming to Harvard. When they came to campus, they ran to the bookshop and stocked up on Harvard gear. My grandparents were proud that I was at Harvard, and a lot of that pride had to do with the safety afforded by nearly universal brand recognition. Harvard was as big as Nestlé and Coca-Cola, maybe bigger. My grandparents now possessed something loads of American citizens wanted, something valued and rare that had evaded others but not them. But seeing them wear any Harvard merch crushed me. When my grandmother wore a pink HARVARD GRANDMA baseball hat, she moved differently, she was more bouncy and giggly, relaxed. I suspected people were nicer to her when she wore Harvard gear. Maybe people acknowledged her presence in an elevator, said, *Good day, ma'am. What floor?*

The exhibit was held on the fourth floor, the Latin American wing. Under Dr. Murphy's leadership and star power, the exhibit had been envisioned as a multimedia celebration of the khipu. At the far back, near the yearlong Day of the Dead exhibit, stood a Peruvian flute ensemble made up of five men in ponchos, embroidered belts, and chullos, the Andean knitted hat with earflaps, playing pan flutes and charangos. One installation involved a television playing a video called *The Sound of a Forgotten Memory*, which sounded like a piercing static. There was laughter and flash photography coming from the photo booth, where visitors were invited to pose next to a human-size khipu made of alpaca wool.

Some khipus looked like angel hair rainfall, others looked like baby mobiles, some looked like festive necklaces, some like three little sprites in a trench coat hiding under a lot of hair. I sympathized with the codebreakers. Imagine being so close and yet so far. It must drive them crazy. Unless it is read, a book is just an object. There are no holy texts without believers to read them.

Nathaniel was there, but we did not talk. We made eye contact once, by accident, and otherwise did not acknowledge each other. Nathaniel and I hadn't spoken since the incident involving my throwing myself out of his moving car, nor since the incident involving his father and Martha. The explanation I gave my grandparents about the scratches on my face is that I fell while skiing, and they had no idea what skiing looked like or what kinds of injuries you could get skiing, and neither did I, so the excuse worked all around.

My grandfather walked around the Peabody like he was interested in making an offer to buy it. I saw him look pensive in front of a khipu. I wasn't sure he could understand the accompanying label, but it seemed more of a salute than an information-gathering stance.

"Those greedy Spaniards. What do you think happened to all of the gold?"

I told him I didn't know, all I knew was what I learned in class, which was that the Inca people threw the gold into the river so that the Spanish could not have it.

"Good," he said, then walked away again.

Dr. Deborah Murphy took the floor for her opening-night address.

"Hello? Hello?" Dr. Murphy checked her mic. "Hi. Hello. I'm Dr. Deborah Murphy. I appreciate you all being here with us tonight."

The room fell silent, and she began with Harvard's official land acknowledgment.

"First, let us pause to remember that Harvard University is located on the traditional and ancestral land of the Massachusett, the original inhabitants of what is now known as Boston and

Cambridge. We pay respect to the people of the Massachusett Tribe, past and present, and honor the land itself, which remains sacred to the Massachusett People."

"Is this a prayer?" my grandmother whispered.

"No. Well, kind of. But no. You should still act like it's a prayer, though."

That is how they knew to stand still, heads bent, feeling somber.

"We're here in celebration of the khipu, one of the most enduring, enigmatic, and enchanting mysteries of South America and, I would argue, the world. This exhibition is inspired by a single khipu that I discovered just a few years ago. Here was a khipu that had been protected by Inca descendants for centuries, locked away in a secret chamber, looked after by generations of indigenous folks in the highlands. The mayor of that village read an article about me in *Time* and he contacted me, invited me to look at the khipu and see what I could tell him about this sacred object that was a mystery even to him. When the villagers told me to take off my gloves because I had been chosen by the khipu, I became quite emotional. These campesinos trusted me to come to their community, they trusted me to take pictures, and they even allowed me the privilege of touching the khipu. I was the first outsider who had ever laid eyes on it. Trust me, I know how lucky I am, but not all fieldwork is this transcendent of a moment. Most of it is false leads, endless spreadsheets, and email chains about permits. Most of it can feel thankless and disappointing. But I believe those moments of serendipity and transcendence are the ancestors calling to us to tell us their stories. Join me in envisioning these countless untold stories. These knots, these twists, these fibers, are reaching out to us from the past and our hands can't quite reach back. But thanks to the work of everyone here tonight, we're one step closer."

The Ituraldes took the Chinatown bus home together. I sat next to my grandmother and my grandfather sat behind us. None of us talked. My grandfather spent the whole time napping, and my grandmother looked through issues of *Vanity Fair* and *Hello!* magazine that she had borrowed from the library. After the first hour, she fell asleep, too. They had made this four-hour bus ride twice in one day to support me. This is a sweet memory for me. I felt like we had just spent hours playing Frisbee at the beach. A sunny, warm, cozy kind of love. I didn't feel it often, but once in a while it would hit me. I loved them.

My grandma and I woke up the next day and did not find my grandfather in the apartment. This was normal. Every weekend, when he woke up before us, he ran down to the bodega to get a newspaper and a coffee. If the Dominican bodega was crowded he went to the Egyptians' bodega for a coffee and a bacon egg and cheese—that was a few blocks away.

But the afternoon came and went and he was still missing. What if my grandfather had dementia and he had just started walking? We would never find him. We'd find his body in the East River. A construction site might have collapsed on him, or he could have had an unfortunate and unexpected encounter with a rabid animal of some kind, or a deadly spider. Maybe a tree fell on him. I went downstairs to the Dominican guys at the bodega to ask if they'd seen him.

"He came here early, maybe six A.M. I remember because he was outside when we came to open."

He was not picking up his phone. The calls were going to voicemail.

"Where do you think he went?" I asked my grandma.

"It's possible he went to watch people play volleyball at the park. But the games end in the afternoon. He would be back by now."

I went into my room and threw myself on the bed. I instinctively reached for my laptop as though there was anyone for me to write to for help. There on the desk, on top of my laptop, was a small white box. A black satin ribbon—one of my hair ribbons—was looped twice around the box, knotted three times and tied into a lovely bow.

Have you ever ordered takeout and received your food packed lovingly inside plastic bags tied with half a dozen knots and a bow no gymnastics coach could find fault in? Are the knots impossible to undo, making the food only accessible with kitchen scissors or a serrated knife? Those plastic bags were probably tied by Ecuadorians.

Right underneath the lid there was a note, folded just to size. The note was on graph paper, my grandfather's paper of choice.

My beloved daughter—

I'm an old man and I've been here too long. It's time for me to return home. Take care of your grandmother.

Abuelo.

Also inside the box: the gold chain my grandfather wore throughout military school. Right away, I thought of two possible interpretations. The romantic one, that he wanted me to wear his chain as a memento to remember him by. And the practical one, that he believed I could have it pawned if we needed the money.

The last item in the box was a scrap of khipu roughly the size of a Penguin Modern Classic. It sat on a little bed made out of his nicest Kingdom Hall ties. I immediately recognized it from the Peabody's exhibit, and squeezed my eyes shut trying to remember its provenance. I was pretty sure it was on loan from a private collector in Upstate New York whose great-uncle had bequeathed him some incredible things, one of which was this khipu and another of which was a little red knitted woolen hat with earflaps so small it could have only belonged to an Andean infant.

There's this story in the Old Testament about the sons of Noah; the old man was naked and one of his sons saw him and instead of covering him up, he ran to tell his brothers. As soon as they heard that their father was found naked, those brothers went over there to cover him up. I am not sure why their father was naked and could not cover himself up and I suspect I do not want to know because the Old Testament is very strange. The point of the story, as I learned it, was that seeing the father in all his nakedness and gawking at him with his armor off was an act against God.

I closed the box, slipped it under my pillow, and went into the kitchen to pass the note to my grandma.

"Lord, please let this be a nightmare," she cried.

My grandmother went absolutely ballistic, opening and closing closets and drawers, throwing his clothes on the floor, throwing them in the air. She threw one of his Kingdom Hall shirts as forcefully as she could, and it just fell on top of her. She found every single photo album and ripped my grandfather's face out of all the photos. After that, she left the photo albums to do some damage to his chessboards. I knelt on the floor to see what I could salvage. The picture of me at five years old, meeting my grandparents at LaGuardia, both of them carrying flowers and teddy bears. She had ripped that one to shreds. She came to me and cried in my lap, and I soothed her and soothed her until I yelled at her to snap out of it.

I could not remember a time when I did not want to die. But now I no longer felt like dying. The worst had happened, and here we were.

He took nothing with him. I looked around the apartment and every object in it suddenly felt charged with sentimental value he had overlooked. It hurt me deeply to know he hadn't taken anything. I understood: If I was leaving everyone behind, I wouldn't take anything that reminded me of anyone, either. But I was tired of being so easily able to provide context for everything he did that hurt me. He really did take nothing.

My grandmother fell asleep in the living room, surrounded by shreds of paper, chess pieces, broken glass and porcelain.

I had no idea how he stole the khipu. From the very beginning, my grandfather and my grandmother jointly agreed to tell me only what I needed to know, and even less than that. For all of my grandfather's dinnertime lectures, he could be fantastically opaque with a flexible relationship to the truth. If you put a gun to my head and asked me for any 100 percent factual information about Latin America, the only information I would be able to give you would come from stuff I've read from Jon Lee Anderson in *The New Yorker*. If you have questions for me about Ecuador, you're better off asking him. I also don't know *why* my grandfather stole the khipu. Maybe he stole the khipu from the exhibit just to fuck with me, one last game of chess before he hung up his cleats as my grandfather. Or perhaps I had underestimated his English again, and he understood every single thing Dr. Deborah Murphy said the night of the opening, and it ate away at him, just as it had me.

Immediately upon setting foot in the Andes, the Spanish set out to compile a history of the Inca Empire and of the Andean region. From the very beginning, they were interested in studying the language, the clothing, the flora, the fauna. They wanted to document everything. It was this initial impulse to document the world that they were themselves destroying that made my blood boil. So I rooted against the khipu codebreakers. I hoped that they would never unlock the secrets of the khipu. I hoped that for them, it remained an unfulfilled longing. There were consequences to empire.

✳ ●

Byron sent me his rough cut. I had butterflies in my stomach. This was way better than a boy in a band writing a song about me. I thought about Delphine and what she said about doing trauma porn with Byron Wheeler. I hoped this would vindicate me in her eyes. I watched hungrily, excited to see what I looked like through the eyes of an auteur.

Because so much of it was footage of me crying, Byron had cut it staggered like a silent film. The score was dark and psychedelic. I hadn't paid much attention to the lighting when we were filming but I remembered the transparent-blue sheets, and it was clear now that I was meant to be bathed in blue. The effect was slightly seedy, as if I had been filmed in a motel by the highway or at a strip club. My wishes had come true. I looked beautiful. What would happen to me when I got old? What would happen when men got tired of my whimsy and began seeing me the way they saw my grandparents, not bathed in menthol blue or Prussian blue or the blue from the Book of Lamentations. Like a pest and a parasite. What then?

To: Byron Wheeler
From: Catalina Ituralde
Subject: A note
7:32 P.M.

Dear Byron. I'm going through a lot right now with my grandpa and I don't think I'm in a good headspace to proceed. Can we just pause this for now? I'm sorry if I've disappointed you.

Byron did not respond for several days. I took his silence to mean he was mad, but he was handling his feelings privately, which is something I heard adults did sometimes.

To: Catalina Ituralde
From: Byron Wheeler
Subject: Re: A note
6:07 A.M.

All I want is for you to be healthy and happy. Thanks for letting me know. Let's be in touch soon.

⋆ °

Thanks to my grandfather's departing gift, I was probably marginally connected to a crime now, so I sought counsel with Don Luis.

As soon as you get off the 7 train at 82nd Street–Jackson Heights you know you're in a different part of the city. It has its own climate, a lot of Latines, Southeast Asian people, East Asian people, lots of Orthodox Jewish families and our newest neighbors, white kids from Vassar who couldn't afford to live anywhere else and still have enough expendable income to live by their values. Owning *just one really good pair of everything* doesn't just *happen.*

"Hello, Don Luis?" I said, knocking on the door after opening it. "Sorry to drop by without calling you." His tiny office was packed and bustling with people.

"Don't worry about it, niña," he said. "Why don't you take a seat? I'll be with you in just one little moment."

There was no place to take a seat, so I sat on the carpeted floor against a wall. He was looking over someone's taxes.

"Niña, let's just get started. What can I do for you?"

"I prefer to wait until I can tell you in confidence. It's a bit delicate."

So I waited another hour, and then Don Luis got up, turned the OPEN sign on his door the other way, so the office officially looked closed. Then he leaned back in his chair and said, "How can I be of service?"

"My grandfather self-deported and maybe before he left he stole something from a museum I work at. I don't know for sure he did it. I don't know what happened at all. All I know is one day we woke up and he was gone, and this was on my bed." It all came out at once. I got up and placed the box in front of him. He opened it carefully, looked down briefly, then looked away, out of concern for modesty.

"If I were you," he said, "I would get rid of it. If you return it, they'll have you file a report with the police and that could complicate things for you, your grandfather, everybody. There is also, of course, a risk in keeping it."

I thanked Don Luis for his advice and asked for his discretion.

"My secrets will die with me," he said solemnly. Don Luis's natural manner of speaking made him sound like he was playing himself in a biopic. He walked me to the door and patted me on the back sympathetically.

"Before you go, niña—however you decide to get rid of it, don't tell anyone. Don't tell your grandmother. Don't tell me."

I nodded.

I walked to the train station trying to take in Jackson Heights as if I would never see it again. I felt overcome by a deep love for the city, its streets. I thought about Isabella Gomes and the plates she restored so lovingly for the exhibit. They were displayed alongside the khipu to illustrate the extent to which art in the early sixteenth century was shaped by exploration, conquest, and colonization. The plates Isabella worked on were probably from the mid- to late 1500s, found somewhere in the "Viceroyalty of Peru," which is what the Spanish originally called the territory they had just conquered. Spanish blue-and-white porcelain is arresting for its craftsmanship, but what's most striking about it is the co-existence of Chinese and Islamic motifs like blue dragons and arabesque lines alongside Spanish heraldic symbols like coats of arms and fleur-de-lis. It was a hodgepodge of influences and references all made possible by violent encounter.

I felt like there was hope for us.

On my way to the train station, I stopped by a street memorial that looked new and made the sign of the cross instinctively. Stapled to a pole was a thickly laminated picture of a pretty young girl with red flat-ironed straight hair, arched eyebrows, and long eyelashes. It looked like a graduation picture, and above it was a crown of dahlias and red roses, a stuffed elephant, and white and black plastic rosaries. I had seen so many of these street memorials. Each time, I tried to memorize the faces of the girls, teenage runaways and sex workers and trans women, women who had definitely not died of natural causes. There were so many of them. I knew too much to keep on walking. I didn't know who this girl was, but it didn't matter. The point is, someone put their hands on her.

EPILOGUE

NATHANIEL AND I agreed we were better off as friends, we were graduating anyway. We had sex one last time, one for the road, a heartfelt farewell. I said another guy's name. Oh, don't be mad at me. One can only hear so many thoughts on the body of Eva Perón.

Delphine and Kyle moved to New York after graduation. Delphine started med school at Columbia, and Kyle joined TV's third-most-popular late-night show as a writer. Seeing how my grandfather just disappeared overnight scared Delphine with good reason. She had already lost one parent and didn't want to be too close to my grief, so she kept her distance and I gave her space, but when we both got iPhones we discovered that we could just play pool over iMessage and it would feel like a hug and we didn't need to talk.

My grandmother and I learned to shovel our own snow and put in and take out the AC window units twice a year. We prepared for hurricanes, and we watched enthusiasm for fascism take over Western countries one by one without my grandfather at the head of the dinner table in his old military beret explaining how to handle men who want to be kings.

My grandmother looked for work immediately, like she'd been waiting for this moment her whole life. She asked everyone in the congregation for leads. She made flyers for babysitting and pet sitting. She did research on Craigslist. One morning, she woke me up to ask me to find her yoga videos on YouTube. I sleepily pulled up a video on my laptop, then curled up in the love seat and went back to sleep as she tried yoga for the first time. Another morning, she woke up and said she wanted to get her GED. Another morning, she woke up and said she wanted to go back to school to properly learn English. None of those realizations could apparently wait until I was awake. A new chapter was starting. There were days to be had.

As for me, I tutored rich kids. Byron had gone to college with the CEO of a tutoring company. He introduced us over email and explained, confidently, succinctly—and technically true!—that I was in between immigration paperwork, and for now, it was best to pay me in cash. The request came from Mr. Hollywood himself, someone who would have no reason to fraternize with illegal immigrants. Nepotism was fucking amazing. I already had one job lined up: twin boys from the Upper West Side who were very, very bad at essay writing.

I finished my thesis—*An Oasis of Horror in a Desert of Boredom: Death Tourism and Roberto Bolaño.* I did not win a prize for it, but I did hand it in. I lost my mind a little after that. I definitely did not call the therapist Professor Sandoval told me about. Not for another ten years. I had suffered for so long, and I wanted to get better, just not yet. Francisco Ituralde was the third father to leave me, and I was only twenty-one, I was three for three, I was getting a Harvard diploma, and my bangs were growing out nicely. The

world was my oyster. I had been abandoned, sure, I could do nothing about the fact that I had been abandoned, but I could turn this
ship around, make lemonade out of lemons, I could become the
most famous abandoned girl in the world. Out of all the abandoned
girls in the world, I could be their valedictorian.

IN LOVING MEMORY OF VANESSA GUILLÉN

(1999-2020)

ACKNOWLEDGMENTS

I WANT TO THANK my editor, Christopher Jackson. Girls think they want dads, but what they need are editors. Your trust in me as a person and a writer set me free. It is the honor of my life to get to work with you.

To my team at One World: Lulu Martinez, Avideh Bashirrad, Raaga Rajagopala, Carla Bruce-Eddings, Andrea Pura, Tiffani Ren, Sun Robinson-Smith, and Greg Kubie. Your love for this book sustained me during the many sleepless nights when I couldn't write a word because the world had gone to hell and nothing seemed to matter. Your love for the book mattered, and it fueled me. Thank you.

Thank you to my team at CAA: Via Romano, Crystal Caicedo, Berni Vann. I am indebted to my agent, Mollie Glick. Mollie, you did not give up on me during times I would have given up on myself. You are steadfast, the heavy ocean anchor to my little paper boat.

Thank you to my friends for their unrelenting support. I love you all very much! Quiara Alegría Hudes, Arlly Pinos, Christopher Kramaric, Rosa Salazar, Adam Berkwitt, Raquel Limonic, Stacia Peters, Aleen Keshishian, Diane Guerrero, and Jonathan Blitzer. My deepest love and gratitude for the Zemach-Bersins, the Alroys, the Zemach-Lawlers, and Anne, Eytan, Gili, and Zoe.

Thank you to Selena Gomez for believing in my voice.

Thank you to Juno Birch and her genius.

Thank you to Jon Franzen for his kindness and his wisdom and his general goodwill toward the parking lot birds.

Thank you to my mom and dad, and to my brother. You have my whole heart.

Thank you to Talya, my protector, the only person in the world I actually like. Thank you for teaching me what an outline is and for lending me your brain during all our editing and brainstorming sessions. I will always remember them as some of the happiest times in my life.

ABOUT THE AUTHOR

KARLA CORNEJO VILLAVICENCIO is the author of the National Book Award finalist *The Undocumented Americans*. Her work, which focuses on race, culture, and immigration, has appeared in *The New York Times, The New Yorker, Vogue, Elle, n+1, The New Inquiry,* and *Interview,* and on *This American Life.*

Instagram: @karlarrriot